About the A

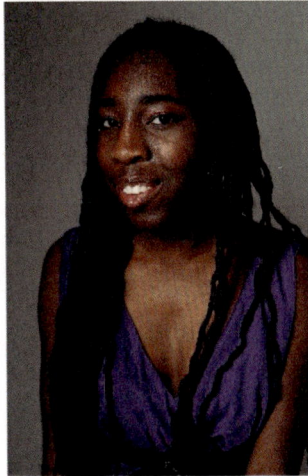

Judetta Whyte is an LLB Law graduate from Durham University. She was born in Edmonton, North London, and is of Ghanaian descent. Judetta aspires to be a Civil Rights Barrister after graduating from university. She is incredibly passionate about advocacy, writing, spirituality, community service, academia and raising mental health awareness. Additionally, she perceives her faith as the most predominant factor within her life and is dedicated towards sharing it with others whilst actively initiating and promoting justice within society. She hopes that *Perpetual Limitations* will provide a firm foundation towards implementing this.

Perpetual Limitations

Judetta Whyte

Perpetual Limitations

Vanguard Press

VANGUARD PAPERBACK

A CIP catalogue record for this title is available from the British Library.

ISBN 978-1-83794-493-4

This is a work of fiction. Names, characters, businesses, places, events and
incidents are either the products of the author's imagination or used in a
fictitious manner. Any resemblance to actual persons, living or dead, or actual
events is purely coincidental.

*Vanguard Press is an imprint of
Pegasus Elliot Mackenzie Publishers Ltd.*
www.pegasuspublishers.com

First Published in 2025

**Vanguard Press
Sheraton House Castle Park
Cambridge England**

Printed & Bound in Great Britain

Dedication

This book is dedicated to anyone feeling empty or low and seeking more within their lives. Whether it is searching for the right solutions, directions, or remedies towards making peace within their current relationships and past and present struggles or hoping for better circumstances to come. I intend to use this book as a bandage for all internalised wounds, for individuals to feel united within their own suffering and seek solace as a source of joy and serenity through endless compassion and support.

Acknowledgements

I'd like to thank God for constantly providing glimmerings of hope and guidance within my life. I'd also like to thank my closest friends and family who never stopped believing in me, particularly during my most challenging trials. I'd also like to thank Pegasus Publishers for offering me this opportunity to share my views, visions and insights with the world.

Foreword

'All that ever was and all that is revealed is not known to man, nor ever will be known to man. Man can only see and comprehend what is in his limited physical and mental realm of understanding and capability; anything beyond that must be shown to man through the spirit of God that is within man, and a man can only realise that knowledge through his devotion to God. All things will resolve back into the Father from whence it came; each will resolve back into its own roots.' Clarence G. Wilson

Prologue

She stood there, aimless. With an open heart and a subsisting spirit, she gradually lifted her eyes upwards, staring intensely towards the endless void of the midnight sky. It was towering above her like a grandiose collection of jewels, formulating their own separate constellations, intertwining and culminating within a metaphysical connection. An accumulation of the forces of nature were leaning beside her until suddenly, a gentle pause instilled within her. She continued to stand as a combination of rays of light and convergence rapidly extinguished her vision. 'It's not time,' she whispered to herself, desperately trying to comprehend her immediate lack of control. 'IT'S NOT THE RIGHT TIME!' she exclaimed and kneeled on the floor resembling the verge of oblivion, bursting into a bitter cycle of tears...

Chapter 1

Samira had always been regarded as different. But then again, Samira had always experienced a "different" kind of life. Physically, from an outside glance, she appeared disabled. She was a paraplegic, hard of hearing, had incredibly poor vision and was shorter than average height. Yet internally, her mind was racing with a multitude of thoughts. Additionally, she encompassed a vivacious spirit that was desperate for adventure and a chance to escape. She longed towards searching for a chance to liberate herself from the physical discrepancies and missed opportunities which burdened and prevented her from experiencing true amelioration in life. Everyone disregarded her. She was a typical social outcast. But despite the grandiose misfortune targeted towards her, both from external influences and realistic circumstances, she remained somewhat hopeful. All the odds may have been stacked against her; perhaps life's trials intended to eliminate her presumably weakened spirit. Even so, she refused to allow personal problems to further diminish her "damaged" physical appearance. Similarly, she was unwilling to permit all the internal anguish laden on her dejected soul prevail and define her entire existence.

'So, explain to me, Samira, how can one possibly choose the right answer within this hypothesis, despite the supposed solution beckoning towards various options of moral intentions?' the Sage asked, her aquamarine blue eyes illuminating sharply as she mentioned the word "moral".

Samira continued gazing blankly at the window outside. She blinked a few times as her highly advanced hearing aids took the time to fully process the Sage's question. It was a meagre day in terms of the weather; it was not too bright, not too sunny, but nevertheless a clear sky with a few grey clouds scattered around.

'I believe that the right question to ask is not necessarily whether one's solution should be dependent upon the level of morality exemplified by different individuals, but rather whether their willingness to search for the right answer in the first place is most significant?'

She mumbled as she blinked rapidly with a forlorn expression, bowing her head towards the ground.

The Sage leaned forward enthusiastically and displayed a warm, tender smile. 'That is correct.'

Samira continued to stare blankly, processing the Sage's response. As Samira experienced partial deafness, she was inclined towards focusing more closely on the remnants of phonetic expression, which was further supplemented by one's facial expression rather than a word's predominant symbolism, dependent on its specific context. Despite her reluctance towards offering the Sage direct eye contact, Samira was familiar with the Sage's dictation and tone. Hence, she managed to comprehend the exact significance of those particular words. This demonstrated another reason explaining why she was unable to completely understand how others instantly dismissed her as "incapable" or "retarded". As this strongly contrasted with a general perception of her natural stimuli, which surpassed capabilities demonstrated by the average person.

Perhaps, sometimes, it's better to assess your own worth introspectively... Often, other people are not interested in unravelling the onion further; they would rather witness events from a surface level, she constantly thought to herself.

'What are you thinking about, Samira?' The Sage decided to cease the lesson temporarily rather than holding it in abeyance permanently, as she was strongly aware of Samira's frequent distractions. She would often chuckle to herself in amusement about how much the eighteen-year-old lived inside her head. Yet, Samira's highly distinguished sense of awareness in light of her surroundings never ceased to amaze her.

Samira retained her blank expression and mustered a glance towards the Sage's direction.

'I need to go,' she stated.

'Go where?' the Sage responded, her expression becoming slightly startled.

'There's some kind of force, drawing me in, like a current dragging a drowning child into the sea. I must follow this current.'

'What exactly do you mean, Samira?'

'It's hard to describe... yes, it's genuinely unfathomable, but I sense something granting me a natural tendency or an unprecedented impulse possibly to leave.'

The Sage looked at her, astounded with her lips quivering, baffled at Samira's sudden divergence from reality.

'Are you s-sure?'

'I just do not understand why.'

Samira moved off her seat and started walking towards the exit of the library, her hands brushing gently across every chair and piece of wood for balance and to provide stability.

'I must go,' she stated with a slightly more assertive tone in her voice.

As soon as she mentioned those words, a grand explosion ignited in the distance whilst a colossal, thick cloud of smoke with cinders dispersing within the air was suddenly visible.

'I've seen this before... come with me.' The Sage quickly grabbed hold of Samira's hand and teleported into a hidden passageway as Samira silently obeyed.

Chapter 2

She awoke within her slumber, almost completely disinhibited. Everything that she had desired and longed for within her life gradually slipped away from her grasp. Tiny clouds spiralling within evanescent pockets of dust began rotating as the thick cloud of black smoke engulfed the entire landscape of the terrace. It resembled an atmosphere overwhelmed by oblivion. No symptom of hope, desire, life, light or even speculations of starlight remained visible. Within her reach, all that remained were her thoughts. Her internal monologue consisted of a cacophonic chorus, echoing sighs of moderate doubt and overbearing shrieks of woe. The sounds rapidly escalated, comprising a piercing screech, and then slowly lulled down into silence.

To her surprise, Samira realised that her thoughts had been replaced by words. The wind and the air surrounding her swept up canticles of dust, becoming thicker and thicker, swaying in an elegant motion. She began speaking voraciously and vociferously in a multitude of languages, pitches, and tones. She bent down in a dramatic motion, taking a pause to recollect everything nouvelle about these circumstances. She sighed in atonement, dusted herself off the ground and opened her eyes.

For once in her life, she became capable of seeing.

Not only seeing but visualising the hidden sights of human life in an extraordinary manner, transcending the limits and capabilities of the average human person. It was as if she had switched bodies with an able person but had also been endowed with enhanced prowess, agility, and strength, as well as heavy doses of energy, striking her accumulatively all at once.

As her mind expanded more and more into a rapid stream of consciousness, she acknowledged practically every thought, sound, and circumstance, including the wind brushing against her hair, whilst recollecting within a swift motion of an enraptured and synchronised form of tranquillity. Samira could not help but feel as though she was not only at one with nature but emboldened by its presence and all external forces swirling around her, suddenly entering the depths of her soul.

For once, she was not bound by the concepts locked within her imagination. Instead, she sought towards envisioning a reality that was predominantly engulfed with unknown mysteries.

Her uncertainty had been exchanged with the doubt which lay amidst the prevalent certainties of the circumstances confronting her. But what was most absurd about this remarkable experience was that she had never requested or longed for any of it. Being visually impaired made perfect sense to her. She never intended to expose herself to the insidious horrors of daily society.

Likewise, being profoundly deaf was something that she regarded as a hidden strength that enabled her to focus and prioritise her own thoughts in a more significant fashion. She may have consistently relied upon her hearing aids to observe and become more connected towards the explicit thoughts of others, but she ultimately regarded it as something that accentuated her unique nature. It was a source of protection against becoming further diminished by the expectations that society had plunged upon her.

'No...' she whispered, 'surely this cannot be rendered as my destiny?' Her eyes darted around in mere disbelief as she was held still, completely isolated within the void location. She slowly took two steps forward, astonished at how, for once, there was no longer a persisting pain within her thigh as she bent her knee. For once, she was able to stand without a significant delay, without much thought or required assistance.

Hmm... she thought, *this is what I know to be regarded as true independence, and yet people complain about being unable to arrive at their destination at a certain time...*

It was true that Samira found herself developing in a highly technologically advanced world. A world where people were no longer paying attention to the wondrous beauty encapsulated within the natural world. A world where people constantly relied upon entertainment and completing activities rapidly whilst withholding themselves from interacting on an interpersonal level. This unfortunate truth had always left Samira incredibly perplexed and despondent. She was already frustrated about the quality of her disfigured condition in comparison to almost everyone she knew. But what left her more discontent was the fact that everyone around her was *choosing* to become increasingly detached as well as less wary and cautious. The prevalent ignorance showcased by humanity circulating every depth of her world was overbearing. Hence, losing all patience was justifiable.

'Samira...' she instantly snapped back to reality, detaching herself from her thoughts, as she suddenly became determined to comprehend the origins of this mysterious voice.

'Samira'...

'Samira...'

'The original Samurai...'

Samira's heart stopped thumping for a second as her eyes widened in a strange dichotomy of terror and embracing comfort. She turned around slowly, mustering a faint smile.

'It's you,' the Sage stated, as her soft voice whispered with reassuring enthusiasm.

Chapter 3

It was mystical moments like these which underlined the significance of reality for Samira. A genuine reality which was enough to appease the naked eye yet simultaneously more than enough to discombobulate anyone to encounter such subliminal insight. Despite the scenery around her being consumed by extreme darkness and morbidity, the only fragments of light present were gentle wisps of air sprinkled with webs of stardust, illuminating every few seconds and dimming every other second. With her newfound sight, it would be expected that Samira should encompass the ability to experience complete awe and wonder at the natural world surrounding her. However, within this moment, she struggled to feel anything. Instead, she was overcome by a pervasion of numbness amidst her astonishment.

Instead, this newfound existence, compounded of sensations and speculations, only reinforced her most sincere doubts. Within this void of creation, she had finally gained the chance to feel, witness and experience the veritable light and compassion perpetuated by the Creator. Yet, instead, she remained isolated, which was generally her most prominent natural sentiment. As her frail figure remained stiff within the presence of the Sage, internally, her limbs, muscles and nerves were crackling with electricity, her thoughts pacing at an even greater speed. The energy intensifying within her was more potent than an active volcano voraciously and vociferously erupting. She remained still as her eyes flared up in exhilaration, darting rapidly towards the sky and the vacant floor below, until she finally paused and gradually gazed down at her hands.

I have all this power, and yet I only desire for less, she thought.

The unknown voice calling her name was indeed the Sage. But within this alternative reality, the Sage had inhabited a new incorporeal form. Rather than encompassing the presence of a rather elderly woman with a white tunic and rigid stature, she had transfigured into a being of light, levitating in a nebulous form with a sphere of gentle heat surrounding her. Her presence resembled a minuscule beam of radiance, gleaming phosphorescence. Her dazzling appearance matched the grandiose crystallised sky, adorned by millions of stars beaming humbly amidst the luminescent splendour of the scene.

The tips of Samira's ears twitched and pricked up with moderate alarm. All at once, she was bombarded with raptured motions flowing from every single particle, angle, and element of existence. She blinked slowly, dazed within a reflective stance, as memories of her past consumed the present moment. The Sage's incorporeal body flickered with light, almost as if she was suffering from an epileptic fit. Simultaneously, a bright light blazed externally within the vast amount of space surrounding the two. It increased in moderation and then gradually simmered down, fading

24

into darkness, whilst thick fog serenaded across the air. Samira suddenly felt a piercing tinge of pain strike against the vessels of her heart on the left side. She winced in severe discomfort as she visualised the memory of isolation. A memory she desperately longed to forget.

A group of eleven-year-old pupils were gathering outside the main classroom of her primary school. They were a mixture of boys and girls, giggling and socialising in every conventional way that you could imagine. Samira begrudgingly joined the group, attempting to showcase a friendly demeanour, only to be inevitably shunned. Within her blind and deaf state, she could not exactly witness the other pupils' reactions towards her, but she could strongly sense and administer their evident disapproval, staring her down in complete contempt. The other pupils sneered and pointed whilst mocking her body posture, lowering their heads and trotting along in a zombie-like state.

Samira, as a young child, was unsure about the best option to react. She could not even relate to the other pupils' mannerisms or ambitions and goals as they were able to sense and experience every fallible essence of human existence. Rather, she was forbidden from doing so. She was nothing more than a burden. She was bound to simply bear all the torment and disgust launched towards her. And there was a minimal chance of change. She was solely *defined* by her own vulnerability.

Even at that age, she was aware that children encompassed extremely fragile and brittle levels of self-esteem. She knew that words had a malleable effect on them, specifically by making or breaking their highly impressionable minds. Nevertheless, she prepared to protect herself by accepting the malicious actions of those in authority towards whom they regarded as uncivilised.

She wondered why... Her thoughts constantly echoed... 'How could it be possible for someone to bear so much pain, merely because of their incapability to reach *"normal"* standards?'

Why was it always necessary for humans to feel compelled to act as if they were omniscient and omnipotent beings, encompassing all the answers whilst consistently emanating perfection?

Moreover, she was frustrated at the concept of even treatment between those who were fortunate and unfortunate against their own will. As if it was likely for healthy, able people to possess the potential to make any sort of mistake without the possibility of being completely exonerated from formulating unsatisfactory decisions, then how could anything relatively become easier for mentally retarded paraplegics?

Everything for people like her was so unnecessarily harsh and difficult. We were all meant to be destined for greatness. And yet, those suffering from severe mortification and insubstantial health were instantaneously destined for destruction.

Chapter 4

Samira had decided to rest upon the surface of a hollow wooden stump which resembled the physical appearance of a willow tree. She bowed her head towards the ground, on the verge of tears as all her internal thoughts spiralled externally, forming a thick cloud, pixelated with various speckles of dust, transpiring in an everlasting circular motion and dispersing into a light pallet of mist. She intended to gulp down the lump growing within her throat as the Sage drew closer towards her, and her radiant figure embodied dignified solace, instantly calming her alarmed and moderately agitated mindset.

'Where are the others?' Samira whimpered, still transfixed within prevalent disbelief at her newfound articulation ability.

The Sage stared at her with a grave expression for a few moments and simply answered, 'They are with us and no longer with us.' She took a few steps away from Samira and turned and glanced wistfully into the distance.

'If anything, only their spirit remains.'

Samira inhaled sharply, and as she exhaled, a bizarre wheezing noise exuded. She blinked rapidly once more, a common habit of hers, and closed her eyes whilst frowning her face, as it was even possible to notice her veins protruding from the surface of her delicate, non-porous skin. Her lips twitched as she regained control of her composure and showcased the logical elements of her personality, overshadowing her naturally creative and poetic expression.

'And yet their souls linger, whether for good or bad, haunting those who likewise linger in the present, paralysed within their own thoughts, prohibited from exploring the unknown or whatever comprises of the "Afterlife" or the Land of the Forgotten as we know it… Until they have reached the point of ultimate escape. Escape for which I have desperately longed for and yet I have always been forbidden from attaining. Instead, I remain here as a living burden, serving no purpose. Utterly void and cast away from any possibility of experiencing human connection. I can only rely on my thoughts as a measure of condolence. As a measure of complete sanity.'

The Sage rapidly turned to face Samira. Externally, it seemed as though she was determined to dispute every element of Samira's interpretation of her own existence. The Sage had a choice between shattering Samira's mindset even further by unveiling the truth or allowing Samira to seek the light within her own dismal thoughts independently. However, the Sage was highly conscious of Samira's common tendencies towards wallowing within her own despair as a form of comprehending the collective pain and trauma her past experiences had pummelled her with. From the outset, the Sage was witnessing the presence of a genuinely broken individual, crippled by pessimism, refusing to reclaim her own happiness. Yet, at the same time, Samira was presently self-conflicted, on the verge of completely surrendering herself towards a malevolent force, desperate to seize every essence of her being, particularly the punctured elements of her soul, for eternity.

The Sage longed to grant Samira the ability to experience eternal happiness and readily redeem herself in the most facile way possible. But Samira already encompassed an ability which would automatically liberate herself from the pangs and slings and arrows of death itself. Regardless of whatever terrifying situation that would confront her, ultimately, she possessed individual autonomy. This ingredient was inaugurated by her own free will which served as the primary essence required for redemption. It manifested within her sole ability to reason and decide upon her own fate. It was the first and last essential authority to save herself. And despite everything, it remained as her final source of hope.

Chapter 5

'Destruction awaits,' the icy expression released from the tip of Sage's tongue was surprisingly not unsettling for Samira.

The young woman continued to glance at the empty floor beneath her dainty feet, completely indifferent. She was determined not to be alarmed by this apocalyptic message.

'Destruction?' Samira almost mustered enough energy to chuckle to herself with amusement, but her stiff, grave demeanour prevented her from doing so. 'What more destruction could be disponible? Considering the damage that humankind has already inflicted upon themselves. This was inevitable; our fate was sealed an eternity ago. I'd prefer total oblivion to occur now rather than never.'

The Sage gazed into Samira's eyes, her aura emanating subtle despondence but predominantly a colossal, heart-wrenching amount of pity and agony towards the girl standing before her. For Samira, this reaction was not alarming in the slightest. She was used to being regarded as nothing more than "damaged goods", which explained the neglect that she experienced from her former foster parents as well as the superficial mannerisms and ideals embedded within her so-called "companions".

She was always obligated to face the world alone, regardless of all the potential circumstances, despite the possibilities and inherent desires of being united and uplifted by people who would truly embrace every disintegrated fragment of her personhood. All that she had ever longed for was for people to recognise her true values and to nurture her own dignity, without the desperation element to protect the downtrodden in addition to those physically incapable of making their own choices. What they failed to understand was the fact that this was due to societal prejudices and treatment instantly depriving individuals with difficulties of their own worth. This would also lead towards their prohibition from accessing regular activities that any individual would take for granted.

These simple activities ranged from standing on a pedestal to see your reflection whilst brushing your teeth, hoping to easily comprehend a teacher's instructions, or actively contributing to a discussion in class as soon as an opinion is requested. Despite Samira exhibiting high aptitude and emotional intelligence, which was showcased by her impressive capabilities of collecting information at incredibly vast and rapid rates with ease, often it took a longer amount of time for her to react appropriately and complete simple activities, including towards other people her own age as well as her elders and moving around with little disturbance. As if dealing with those circumstances wasn't challenging enough, Samira would also have to deal with the mental, emotional, and physical repercussions of her perceived disabilities. Amidst the frustration, as she was often automatically rendered as a "profound inconvenience" within her community. She would have to cope with the frequent stares, the insolent comments and ongoing ignorance. And yet, they had the nerve to declare her as "the problem" even though she was merely minding her own business, trying to live her life personally and peacefully without being overwhelmed by excess pressure.

Even if there was a speck of hope flickering within her, society had rendered it impossible to prepare her for any possibility towards opening her heart to offer and receive genuine human compassion.

Complaining was futile. Protesting was futile. They signified ingratitude. All the odds would always be stacked against her. Despite Samira's efforts towards remaining patient, the quest towards becoming a more understanding, considerate and merciful individual certainly required meticulous attention. She was used to handling abuse, but the profoundly latent emotional scars assimilated within the depths of her heart tissue seriously fractured her relationship with humankind.

'So, you are void of faith and spirit. But you should not allow humanity's transgressions and prejudices against you to initiate your destruction. There is a venomous essence that lingers and is partly embodied and manifested by the colossal spheres entrenched by your sustained fury. That is where evil is derived from. It is an invisible emblem of excessive pride which swiftly erodes your humility and integrity. You must resist temptation...'

'NO!' Samira flung her wrist away from Sage's gentle

hold of her hand as her eyes blazed with intense rage and indignant frustration.

'As if it's that simple to seek forgiveness! Especially as it is highly probable that they'll consider it as a sign of weakness! They were merciless towards me, so they deserve no mercy themselves. They've extinguished every flicker of hope that remained within every cellular molecule of my body, and the depths of the bloodstream affixed within my heart. Tell me, Ma Dame, what is hope for? Why should we long for a better ending or situation when suffering is inevitable? We are consistently imprisoned within the cages and shackles of our own darkness entangled within our lack of reasonable consideration, showcased as pure madness! Moreover, we are further burdened by society's influence dictating our future choices, perceptions, and thoughts. Is there ever really "*a choice*"? Or is everything that we genuinely choose to become of ourselves automatically aligned towards reducing or ameliorating the happiness of others? Spare me your inspirational insights, compliments and optimistic attitude about renewal and transformation. There is no chance of metamorphosis for me. I will resist it. For a while, I believed that there was a chance that people could change. We should break free from fear and our unearthly dependence on material, ephemeral possessions, which are presented as necessary and fundamental for our survival! As I, for one, am unwilling and I choose not to abide by their amenable expectations and aspirations. For there is no need.'

'Your faith is faltering…'

'I will remain persistent. I will always uphold confidence and faith within myself until the very end. However, I am no longer placing humanity above my own desires.' she stated stubbornly.

'Samira, listen to me. If you deprive yourself of altruism, you are only damaging yourself. You will become exactly like them: incredibly self-obsessed, cold, needy, arrogant and petty. You will lose all innovation and only become concerned with the superficial elements of your own existence. Losing your desire to serve humanity involves disposing of all the benevolent parts of yourself, which naturally makes you more attractive. It is like a splendorous garden radiated with iridescent flowers becoming riddled with prudent thorns and stinging nettles, distorting its overall original beauty. Now, ask yourself. Is it worth losing everything for the sake of your warped interpretation of happiness? Samira, you are worthy of so much more than that. Goodness will always remain within you. But only you can activate and acknowledge your own glory by consequently embracing it and inspiring everyone else to do the same.

I am not asking you to avoid listening to your own intuition and internalised inclinations. Humanity is a central element within its own. All that is required to ensure the promise of salvation is dignity, respect, and collective responsibility to be maintained and upheld. In the end, discovering the unity of self in addition to collective responsibility is required to eradicate the Sphere of Restrictions. This must be maintained at all costs, for it is the Creator's will.'

Chapter 6

Samira continued to stare vacantly at her own reflection, a perfectly symmetrical rectangle overflowing with ripples lying on the surface of the deserted land where she remained standing.

She paused, allowing herself to process the Sage's divine wisdom and intellect to settle her disrupted, emotionally volatile state.

Her frustration was often a dangerous tool which she relentlessly struggled to control, but the Sage always would place her back onto the right track. After all, despite the restrictive circumstances around her, Samira's imagination was not only her place of solace and temporary bliss. Instead, she was more settled by the knowledge that she would always be destined for something greater. However, poverty, class division and conflict failed to circumvent that.

'But, Ma Dame... what is the purpose of the restoration of my abilities? If there is a grave threat placing humanity at risk, it should not be of concern as it is outside of my control. I'm not The Creator.'

The Sage smiled meekly. 'It is good that you recognise where your true power lies within the eyes of the Creator. But the Creator has granted you a purpose and you must use your gifts to initiate and embellish this purpose.

Everything may have been created out of nothing, but everything created is designated with a specific plan for *something*. We may not need to be aware of all the reasons why, but all that we can do is use everything that we know now in order to accomplish what is necessary.'

'Actually, I don't think that this is the best idea... I have nothing grand to offer.' Samira continued to look towards the ground, hoping that all her thoughts would dissipate onto the surface.

The Sage was familiar with the demeanour displaced by her student. She was riddled with self-doubt and internalised conflict. For a girl who appeared to be quietly confident, the assured hesitance within her expression was completely visible. The Sage stepped towards Samira again, who continued looking dismally at the ground. The land around them was solemnly still, encrusted with mundane vacancy. The two women stood with measured composure, fully enveloped and enclosed by their long navy-blue tunics, although the Sage's was shimmering with sapphire jewels, glowing directly from the moonlight.

It was the early hours of the morning, precisely three a.m., (although for Samira, it seemed to be a lot longer), and darkness continued to pervade amidst their surroundings. From a distance, it appeared to be the Blue Hour, which often occurs when the blue wavelengths and subtle hues projected by the sunlight dominate due to Chappuis absorption, but rather the setting resembled the nautical stage of twilight, primarily dusk or dawn or as the French preferred to call it between the sheep and wolves.

Regardless of the evening presence held within the

current atmosphere, Samira's enduring resilience remained as she was focused on persevering. She remained uncertain about the instructions imposed upon her impending quest, and moreover, she was determined to avoid it. She had experienced enough danger, abuse and adversity within her lifetime, consisting of eighteen years. Hence, she was unwilling to surrender and renounce herself that easily. But broadening her horizons and fighting against the unknown wasn't particularly daunting for her. Rather, the most terrifying aspect was the prospect of change.

Throughout most of her life, before her parents went missing in action, Samira was not so severely disconcerted by little bouts of instability; instead, she would be able to handle surprises to no avail and cope with the inevitable, dynamic aspects which life entails. She would accept change as a necessity. But as soon as she had to muster all the courage within her life – the greatest change of all – managing life on her own, all the exquisite pieces and magical moments which had culminated within the living masterpiece fermented within her photographic memory suddenly became dented and ruptured. Her initial idealistic attitude has been replaced with pure nihilism. Her upbeat, vivacious personality had faded like a colourful painting being left in the sunlight and instead, she became dismal, disillusioned and irrevocably misanthropic.

The trauma of her parents' loss had profoundly affected her inhibitions and interactions with others, particularly as she was only eight years old at the time, intending to live a normal life alongside and in correspondence with her disabilities. Her parents had always encouraged her to display kindness to others, to follow the Golden Rule of loving her neighbour and constantly displaying mercy towards those who intentionally caused harm. She listened and understood and tried to suppress her alternative motives. She remembers how her father used to say: '*Our actions may be damaging, but it is our thoughts which are the "deadliest".*' She sighed and nodded to herself in approval, for she could not allow her emotional intensity and irrational preconceptions, based on pure malice and retributive desires, to destroy her poor state. She believed that love was a universal force. Hence, there should be no exceptions, and no specific type of person should be designated to love; it should be a joint effort. However, the joint effort can only be initiated if we choose to love primarily as our ultimate, effective individual choice within all circumstances.

Since her parent's disappearance, Samira had raised herself independently as she did not want to be regarded as the "Pity Project" of society or to be utilised as a source of comfort towards those who only displayed care and affection for their own personal gain and attention. It was only a couple of months after that she was able to meet the Sage after she had encountered her, washing her hair by the lake, sometimes on a random evening. Ever since that moment, the Sage had been Samira's acquaintance and teacher for many years, acting as her foster parent and guidance counsellor.

Here, the Sage was once again remaining her comfort

and bedrock during a critical time of need.

'My dear, even the most minuscule actions can formulate the greatest circumstances. You must believe that something greater lies out there for you that can only be developed from within. You claim that you have faith, but what is faith if it is faltering within moments of fleet?'

Samira glanced upwards to form direct eye contact with the Sage, her eyes glistening with mild hope.

'What must I do to complete this quest?'

'There is a hidden location located two hundred fifty-seven miles from here. We are currently on Earth within the regular dimension, but most of humanity has either been wiped out or bunked away discretely. The impending threat is known as the Third Wave of Destruction; it is entirely natural, so there is nothing physically that we can do without it, but the Creator has designated the responsibility to you, out of thousands, to restore order. You must locate the coordinates of the Sphere of Restrictions and meet directly with the Ahir the Elder.'

'Ahir? The Elder?' Samira blinked rapidly, repeating the Sage's instructions in her mind. She often repeated important information to preserve sanity. It was the trait of a typical perfectionist.

'Yes, he is the last remaining elder among us. Are you ready to complete the mission that the Creator has set out for you?'

Samira smiled gracefully, for the first time with genuine light-hearted passion and assurance since the evacuation began, responding, 'I am ready and willing.'

Chapter 7

It could not be disputed that walking was a somewhat therapeutic activity. For Samira, it resembled a glimpse of liberation. As Samira was born paralysed from the waist down, she had grown up envying those who could walk with ease.

But within this moment, she felt incredibly light on her feet, as if she was at one with the four elements. The fire enkindled within her inner core, igniting the passionate sparks that provide movement. The internal fluid flowed faultlessly within her system, providing her with serene tranquillity. The gravity within the air connected her directly towards the earth beneath her, and even during this time when humanity's position within the universe was not guaranteed, the earth continued to maintain its firm condition, unbroken. Samira hoped that the same circumstance would occur for her, that she would remain composed even whilst drowning within a sea of unbridled chaos. Yet, as she continued strolling in a mostly unfazed fashion, she pondered on the fact that despite being free to go wherever she pleased, there were only a few places that one could explore. The Sage's instructions remained firmly imprinted within her mind. She was determined to find the Sphere of Restrictions, which apparently was the only solution towards resorting back to normality.

But then again, she started to question things... Once she had tracked down the Sphere of Restrictions, *would she return to her natural state? Would perfection finally be implemented within the Creator's plan for humanity? Would the world be dismantled around her and then restored?* Samira always wanted to be certain of the future's possibilities. Often, she would perceive the potential of the future as more prominent than the present moment. She was mildly anxious about her likelihood of success within this mission... What would occur if she didn't make it? Would the Creator simply transfer her responsibilities to someone else? And if so, then what would be the point of her even trying at all? It was trivial thoughts like these that were persistently challenging for her to rid herself of, and yet she knew deep down that she needed to continue, regardless of whether the toxic thoughts remained or not.

As she took more steps on the vast, empty road, she was still astonished at how she was finally capable of walking without wincing in discomfort at a slow pace. As she inhaled the clean oxygen flowing through her lungs, she gazed incredulously at her surroundings with newfound sight. She was rather amused at how it was not so different from what she imagined or intended it to be. People often believed that blindness rendered people incapable of witnessing life or from feeling anything at all, but for Samira, it did not prevent her from dreaming. For someone with an incredibly vibrant imagination overloaded with fantastical abstract concepts, it was more than enough to allow her to experience her own form of reality. *After all, our perceptions are reinforced by emotional inclinations; people often see what they want to see or believe what they would ideally like to believe, even if the truth was clearly prevalent, without any reasonable explanations or empirical evidence defying it*, she thought.

Despite all this, Samira firmly held onto what she regarded as the truth: That humanity is destined for greatness, and no one should be deprived of that. She did not exactly need a majestic external sign from the universe as further support for her beliefs or a miraculous twist of fate to transform her entire worldview, as she knew that faith did not necessarily need to be great to be defined as faith. All that remained essential was upholding authenticity and commitment towards her own intentions in honour of human dignity and actively making the right choices.

Amidst her current solitude, Samira felt further emboldened by an unfathomable, mysterious force. She had grown accustomed to periods of total social isolation, the bouts of loneliness, which would often contribute to an overall depleted mindset. As a social outcast, she simply had to accept these circumstances; it would often only appear once within a blue moon where she would encounter a true companion. Otherwise, she would only be surrounded by individuals who were significantly perturbed by her unappealing state. She was used to people shuddering and recoiling in frustration even before gaining a chance to speak to them or to prove herself. She was blissfully aware of those who would stare at her with a moderate sense of pride and repugnance, pleased that they were able-bodied and weren't confined by the stigmatised labels or attitudes that society had plastered onto people like her, which was difficult to erode entirely. In their perfect vision, she would always be regarded as the problem. As an exemplification of ignominy, she was the only one to blame.

She continued strolling along until a city below appeared within her sight. There was a large crowd infested with a multitude of people, scattering around and meandering hastily like a bunch of wild cockroaches, desperate to feast upon a cavern of litter. The frequency of sound delivered from their voices conjured up a variety of noises, which were all unfamiliar to her prior to her exchange of ultra-sensitive ears, which hitherto were unable to detect even the faintest whisper.

So, this is what it must feel like to be overloaded by sound, she thought, with every little thud hitting her, like a new gust of wind brushing harshly across her cheeks.

Samira continued observing the people within the crowd; many of them were Arabian men in their mid-forties with a ferocious, aggressive expression on their faces. They seemed to be infuriated by something, but Samira was unsure about exactly what. A few of them appeared to be mild-mannered and vividly insecure, fidgeting with their fingertips and glancing around anxiously with their eyes fixated on the ground. They all had different types of builds; some were scrawnier than others, whilst others were more muscular. Nevertheless, they were certainly all in a hurry to evacuate.

Samira continued plodding down the hill,

intentionally aiming to block out all the noise below by focusing entirely on her own thoughts. This was a rather challenging game to play, given how distracting her surrounding area was until her eyes fixated on one younger girl who looked about her age, resting on a tree stump, amidst the crowd. She had pale skin, lightly dusted with freckles as a result of pigmentation over the years. She also had medium-length, wispy, strawberry-blonde hair, enshrined with chestnut-brown highlights with a slightly auburn tinge. Like Samira, she was also rather frail and had a bony appearance, but she was wearing an oversized dark grey hoodie as well as glasses, which was unusual within these given circumstances. As within the universe that Samira had known, contact lenses were almost a compulsory asset for everyone. But the unknown girl stripped them away from her face, observed them and fondled them in her hands until deliberately dropping them onto the dusty floor below and stamped on them with unexpected fury.

Samira continued peering at her from a couple of metres away in surprise and began contemplating whether to engage in conversation with her or not. She strongly disliked company, even if it was with one person. She could just about tolerate it with the Sage, but with other young men and women, especially if they were around her age, she found it disorientating and emotionally exhausting. This was primarily because she instantly would never be able to camouflage amongst her peers, given the fact that she was always seen holding crutches or remaining immobile within her wheelchair. Hence, it would always remain impossible for her to conceal her genuine emotions in addition towards blending in with the crowd. If a performance took place at her school, she would always be in the middle front row so that it wouldn't appear as though she was purposely being disregarded and hidden away from sight solely due to her disabilities and handicapped figure.

Usually, Samira had conditioned herself to remain indifferent, to handle it with patience, and to maintain a calm composure as she would never want to cause further disruption more than what she already lacked control over. That was another privilege that able-bodied people seemed to have over her. It was easier for them to showcase their rage or create a dramatic scene out of pettiness because it wouldn't require extra effort or attention to assist their needs and concerns. It would not elicit further sympathy or feelings of shame and guilt from audience members or other members of the professional faculty involved to question and second-guess whether they are treating someone who is significantly more "disadvantaged" than themselves with an equal level of dignity and responsibility. If so, they failed to consider the extent to which it could potentially damage their reputation rather than using the disabled student as an emblem of diversity or as an active muse for social change.

Whilst it was veritable that Samira longed for people to treat her fairly without extra care, attention or "special treatment" (who would possibly deny the desire to live life freely without constant interference or appearing as though they were a nuisance?), she likewise accepted the likelihood of resistance to social change. Of course, you would inevitably get those people who do not care at all. However, amidst their blinding ignorance, they take advantage of others and belittle them further, as a means of displacing their own heavily ingrained insecurities. On the contrary, you would have people who do care by recognising how you yourself are complete within your own personhood and individuality. Thus, they would respect your privacy and respect you unconditionally, refraining from going the extra mile to suit their own pleasure and internalised gratification, but these people were a rarity. Samira would constantly remain perplexed about *why* this was the case.

Regardless of the psychological and sociological explanations justifying human behaviour, often it wasn't about the causes, consequences, effects, and implications but rather about people's general reticence towards initiating a change and committing themselves to it. However, this was not possible as they were protected by their formulated construction of privilege, which they had historically worked for many years to attain initially to not only gain perfection but ultimate security. Why wouldn't they want things to change? Simply because it was too uncomfortable for them to handle.

At the end of the day, Samira was not fussed or concerned about or even invested in the psychological and scientific explanations for human behaviour, as, ultimately, it wouldn't change things. Humans cannot be programmed or controlled by other humans, only indoctrinated, influenced, or coerced by social pressure or deprived of financial status, which would possibly leave them with no other choice but to obey or climb the social ladder to restore their own seemingly missing sense of self-esteem. But was a scientific explanation or a historically implied convoluted theory about sociological conditions really required to validate human compassion? It was questions like these which frustrated Samira the most. Surely, the source of compassion originated within us? To simply reach out? Surely, evidence for this theory was displayed within knowledge and comfort of alleviation of pain, instilled within a distinct memory, or a loving commitment and general forgiveness which had been exemplified by certain individuals over the course of time?

People often believed that searching for the answer externally or being ratified and validated by empirical evidence was ultimately paramount towards discovering the cure for natural diseases and disasters and fixing our broken, complex nature. But Samira was aware of the truth: that the remedy for restoring internal wounds reinforced by our lack of empathy was unconditional love. Unconditional love, which required no explanation. It had always been embedded within the fabric of our being. She was also determined to become inspired by external forces of nature, such as the everlasting warmth coinciding with rays of sunlight, to ignite and initiate internal connections with others to provide greater reconciliation. Samira could feel the internal turmoil and trauma from her past sufferings grapple against the depths of her lungs, but she understood that genuine companionship was essential at this point when time was running out.

Returning to earth, after extricating herself from the tunnelled thoughts of the tortuous, impenetrable strains of her subconscious, her eyes wandered towards the girl again, sitting on the log with an apathetic expression, appearing as though she was on the verge of giving up everything.

But Samira remembered the Sage's final message of *collective* responsibility, nodded again in agreement and subtle obedience, and began making her way towards her.

Chapter 8

The young girl's light, golden-reddish hair strongly contrasted with the sombre simplicity of her outfit. Her oversized, dark grey hoodie nearly covered her knees and ripped denim jeggings. She continued staring dismally at the surface, glancing every few seconds towards her shattered spectacles, her face shrivelling up with rage, frustration, and wavering despair, almost as though she was torn between repairing the damage she had made or causing even greater deterioration to satisfy herself.

How much we all long for the damage that we have caused to be enough... Samira's thoughts echoed, empathising with the other girl's distress combined with her own dejected mindset.

Samira was only a metre away from her now. She didn't exactly plan on what she wanted to say; she wanted to offer a chance for the other girl to acknowledge her presence instead and feel slightly more at ease before engaging with a stranger. She often never understood why people always rushed towards instantly impressing someone before understanding who they really were primarily. She understood that it was a respectable social convention and a matter of common courtesy and etiquette, but it often meant that we were inclined towards acting and delivering a false impression before revealing our true nature. Rather, we ended up developing a form of deceit and instead feared becoming ridiculed or disregarded if we appeared to be too shy, too loquacious or even slightly awkward. But perhaps this was the way things always ought to be to avoid social deprecation.

Samira strongly disliked the idea of being ostracised but, at the same time, was incredibly frustrated about how she never received credit for confidently talking to strangers outside of her comfort zone to deliberately avoid prejudice or misconceptions, even though the former often prevailed.

Samira glanced towards the girl and extended her hand. 'Hello. Are you all right?'

The girl with the pale skin breathed in heavily and looked up towards Samira. Unashamed of displaying her languid, impoverished state, she looked up at Samira, slightly dazzled, smiling faintly.

'The name is Florence Wynne. I'm just taking a break.' Florence turned her head away from Samira and coughed with a chesty congestion noise bellowing from her lungs; it was almost possible to hear the mucus trapped within her trachea as she clutched her chest, attempting to regain her strength. She spoke with a harsh, deep Southern Californian accent, supported by a flawless level of confidence and eloquence, automatically showcasing her naturally polite, well-mannered, and presumably endearing personality. Samira automatically inferred that she had been brought up by a higher class and had received a good quality of education, even though she paradoxically appeared to be so relaxed despite experiencing uncomfortable physical pain.

As Samira secretly felt inferior to Florence, she wondered how it would be possible to form common ground with her.

'I'm Samira,' she said, her voice becoming quieter after pronouncing the second syllable of her name, as she anxiously treaded her feet whilst desperately trying to maintain a quietly confident posture.

'Samira!' She chuckled to herself. 'What does that mean?'

Samira tried to muster a smile to be polite and responded, 'Actually, it's a name of Arabian origins; it means *evening conversationalist.'*

Florence's eyes sparkled as she listened to Samira's name origins explanation. 'Evening conversationalist?' She laughed again. 'I can tell already that you are quite the talker!'

Those words struck Samira slightly as she felt rather offended. She was used to receiving that reaction whenever people asked for her name origins, but it also hurt because it meant that she was imminently being judged for her apparent misdemeanour. But then again, she believed that the fact that her thoughts were rather vociferous, especially at night, was justified by her name origins. She would choose not to express those thoughts as fervently as those with a more extraverted nature, as she believed that it would be too much for other people to handle especially, for seemingly privileged people like Florence, whose associates would probably silence those who threatened their authority.

Descending from a mixed background comprising of African-Asian heritage and unsure about where she really came from was understandably an attribute that made Samira feel insecure. In fact, it rendered her with the "Other" status as she was not only confused and incredibly conflicted about her identity and where she belonged, but also frustrated about how most of the odds were stacked against her. She would fit in amongst people who also shared her physical characteristics, such as her dark, thick Asian hair and dusty olive skin, but amidst others who clearly were fully aware and proud of their heritage, whether it was European, American, Asian, Australasian, or African, she'd always have to appear strong and confident about her physical appearance, despite her paraplegic state. Around people like Florence, she always took greater caution with her actions and decisions. Otherwise, her own identity wouldn't be carved out and moulded and *defined* by herself predominantly but rather by others who were more self-assured and naturally harnessed greater control.

'That's what they all say…' Samira responded.

She wanted to remain as assertive and authentic as possible; if others were incapable of doing so, she owed it to herself to at least make more of an effort. 'But what about you? What does your name symbolise?'

'Haha, my name? In fact, and in theory, it means "white blossoming flower" But within my life as of now, I have never felt or behaved like a white blossoming flower.'

Samira frowned, growing with inquisition, 'How so?'

'Because I robbed myself of my purity. And not in the way that you would expect. I lived a life endowed with wealth and riches, where everything was promised to me. My parents were incredibly wealthy and influential businessmen. The Wynne's. They practically ran all corporate businesses universally, the super intricate and incredibly lavish buildings with their influence stemming from the encrusted, embellished status founded in Los Angeles. Everything was guaranteed for me. A secure job as their predecessor, being surrounded by elite associates, counsellors, "friends" and colleagues to last a lifetime as their futures were likewise secured by my parent's business. They were untouchable. I was untouchable. I had everything that people had worked excessively for over centuries without even doing anything at all. In fact, by simply being born, our wealth and privilege served as my greatest security. At least that's what I thought, until I realised the truth...'

'Which was?' Samira continued listening, remaining fully attentive and transfixed by Florence's story, her eyes widening in awe and mild discomfort.

'I was trapped. I was prohibited from discovering more about myself and who I really am in a different environment. I was brought up amongst people who had the exact same circumstances and "wonderful" lifestyle as me. They were all living in idle bliss, in their own delusional bubbles, refusing to face the dreaded horrors of the natural world. Refusing to interact with people from urban, metropolitan backgrounds simply because they were regarded as too "different". The thing is, it's not even as though we were flawless angels of the house. Nah, we were all rotten, broken, entirely dysfunctional. My parents were cold and disinterested; they hardly paid attention to me. Instead, they were obsessed with their reputations. They rarely displayed compassion or empathy; they cared more about restoring their finances if we faced a minor incident within the business. Many of my various friends and socialites resorted towards drinking, excessive intercourse and drugs to fill the void that they had created in the first place. I also began to follow their hedonistic lifestyles as I believed that the possibility of change was futile. I'd drink bottles ranging from Tequila to Vodka, to Bailey's to Prosecco multiple times a day. It was my only source of comfort. We'd often smoke weed together and get high to conceal and further blockade our conflicted mindsets, insecurities, and domestic neglect. Until one day, I finally escaped, but to escape I had to hit the peak of mental instability. I was locked up in a mental asylum, and after that, my parents disowned me. I was suddenly left with nothing. Not that I had anything much to compare to in the first place. Either way, I was incarcerated. Either way, I was lost. Until I found my way here…'

Samira remained startled, her eyes widening and her mouth and limbs quivering, trying to process and grasp every revelation that Florence had mentioned. Those circumstances were enough to dissuade anyone, and Florence somehow remained inherently calm.

'So, you were locked up in a mental asylum? What was that experience like?'

'First of all, I was completely deprived of all my

human dignity. And I felt so isolated before, but even more so there. The twisted thing was that they told me that this would be the best place for me. I thought that I would receive loving, respectful, attentive care, but I received none of that. As soon as I entered, they thought that I was some wild beast on the loose, determined to demolish everything.

'I was terrified and fighting for my life; every second felt as though I was on the brink of death. I was just being constantly observed by multiple strangers as if I was some kind of domestic pet, unable to control themselves. I had no privacy whatsoever as they believed that I was too mentally deranged to do anything whilst they themselves were able to continue their lives without constant intrusion or separation from those who loved and knew them the most. What's worse was how they were holding me with tight, firm grips, speaking to me in an ultra-patronising tone. Men and women watched me whilst I slept at night, even stripping me of my garments and lurking over me whenever they gained the chance. What was worse was that whenever I "misbehaved", basically screaming for help, they'd pick me up, hold me down and lock me in a cell, which they disguised as "seclusion" because I was regarded as too "dangerous" to be around. They locked me in that "cell" for over forty-eight hours without access to a bathroom or access to any of my friends or close relatives. I saw no one. And yet, I was only eighteen at the time, completely vulnerable, already disempowered within my mental state. I had never felt more broken than ever within that moment. But that's our civilisation for you…'

'That's worse than awful; you practically experienced living death!' Samira exclaimed.

'And yet, here I am, still surviving. Away from all that, thank goodness, but yes, unfortunately, that's the reality that we find ourselves in. It's a completely corrupt system of power, with only eyes for the privileged. However, privilege doesn't really exist; we only give those who act on merit what we think they deserve because we perceive them as our strong protectors. The most idealised versions of reality. But no, those who truly retain their privilege are those who are lowly and humble and meek.'

Samira nodded in approval. She strongly understood and related to the majority of all that Florence had mentioned and yet it was almost as if they were from alternate universes. Florence was dazzlingly beautiful, sophisticated, and intelligent, yet incredibly tormented and broken. Samira was from a lower-class background, and even with her restored abilities, she still felt powerless, outwardly vulnerable and insecure without a fixed address of belonging. Despite never being surrounded by the controlling, despotic impact of capitalism from a first-hand perspective as much as Florence, at least she would find solace within her isolation and friendship with the Sage. She had always upheld compassion within herself and that ultimately provided her with a reason to continue surviving. For someone as adrift and bewildered as Florence, Samira would not comprehend a reason or rational explanation to continue living; if Samira were Florence, she would have given up on life at the first hurdle, especially when it seemed as though she had lost individual agency... and was literally born into those circumstances.

'So why did you continue?' Samira asked.

Florence's brow furrowed slightly. 'I'm sorry?'

'Why didn't you just give up on everything before you left? Before you spiralled into a serious mental health crisis? Before your parents ever had a chance to shut you out? Why didn't you shut everything else around you down before all the walls around you and within you collapsed first?'

'But you see, I never collapsed. What are you trying to say exactly? Why didn't I take my own life? Is that what you're asking? I contemplated it many times. I feel as though, at times, in significant despair, and where we've lost purpose and are immune towards experiencing or expressing feelings of compassion, that's where we are most likely to do it. But I didn't see the point. Instead, I chose not to fixate on a reason to give up. I think that throughout all the chaotic events that humanity has confronted over time, I couldn't help but also become certain that something greater lies out there somehow. It's difficult to explain but simple to understand. That is, if you truly believe in it, I mean. Somehow, throughout my discomfort, there was a force guiding me, pulling me out of my despair. Call it time, memories, natural beauty; I don't know for sure. But all that I know is that without that particularly alluring force, I wouldn't be here today. And we would not be meeting at this time, or ever really.'

Samira blinked rapidly again, trying to swallow down her tears, consoling herself whilst moving to sit beside

Florence.

Florence turned towards her. 'What about you, though? Have you ever faced difficult circumstances in your life? If so, what kept you going? You seem perfect to me.'

Samira suddenly snapped out of her empathetic, open mindset. 'Excuse me?'

'I said you seem perfect.'

Samira scoffed. 'Perfect? I've never been perfect! In fact, this is probably the most "perfect" I have ever been in my life. I was born paralysed.'

'Oh, I didn't... how insensitive of me...'

'You see, that's what you able-bodied people do. You overload us with guilt and sympathy. You don't know how to act around us, and you always seem to assume as though we're some kind of disease or revolting creature, which is a natural hindrance within society. Isn't that right?!' Samira's voice was intensifying with coiled anger.

'No, I'm sorry...' Florence's face began reddening in appearance as she clutched tightly onto her knuckles, attempting to ease the tension arising between her and Samira – the new stranger that she had encountered.

Samira's eyes suddenly widened, and she began speaking in a softer tone whilst relaxing her shoulders. She then again remembered the Sage's advice about evil and anger and resisting temptation. She remembered how she needed to give into her virtues rather than her vices to succeed. Besides, she didn't want to reinforce the trope relating towards victimisation and oversensitivity concerning a lack of acknowledgement for those in need of serious aid or for those currently surviving verbal and physical harassment. She knew that often explosive tension and anger created further division and conflict, inciting a higher level of discrimination, rather than a valid solution which would tackle the root of these problems. Yelling at Florence, a girl she had only just met, about her ignorance and presumed lack of sensitivity certainly did not help the situation that they were in, let alone provide the space to confide in each other during their greatest time of need.

'Actually, you know what, it's fine. None of us are perfect. Perfection is a myth. I don't think that we were even created to be perfect; I think that we were created merely out of love. And love is complex within itself, but it finds its simplicity in the sense where it's ultimately utilised for the good.'

Florence nodded and said, 'I'm sorry to interrupt… but, if you were born paralysed… then how come you're standing on your own two feet right now?'

Samira stared hard directly at Florence. 'Yes, this is the absurd circumstance that I find myself in right now. I've been instructed to go on a mission by the Creator.'

'The Creator? But I thought that the Creator was not to be revealed until the end of time and was not to interfere with the plans of humanity?'

'I believed the same, but apparently, humanity is in need of an object known as the Sphere of Restrictions to restore order to the corruption that it's caused.'

'And what exactly is the Sphere of Restrictions?'

'Actually, I am uncertain about that. For once, I didn't

question what it was when I became aware of my mission. I was processing multiple proficient changes at that point.'

'Well, that's useful.' Florence sighed, rolling her eyes in exasperation, but was somehow still amused. Samira looked at her blankly but was mildly impressed by her bold personality. She was clearly one of those people who used sarcasm as a coping mechanism with a predominant sense of humour to handle all the bleakness and bizarre nature that humanity has to offer.

Fair enough, she thought to herself. She stood up again, gazing at the horizon line. She had been conversing with Florence about the past for several hours. Although Florence had revealed a great deal of information to her, disclosing her own personal circumstances, worldview and the impact of her past struggles formulating her present character, Samira remained reluctant to open up. It was not necessarily because she felt incapable of doing so or because she did not trust Florence, but rather because understanding her past circumstances, her stance on faith and her vocation within the world was a concept that was particularly challenging for her to grasp. She had not reached a point where she had completely accepted her identity or felt comforted within her faith. Everything had always been off balance for her, and not just because she was formerly disabled. She understood that sometimes things occurred for a reason and that sometimes we were given chances offered by the universe, which incorporated our family, heritage, and traditional background. These chances were intertwined with inclinations towards choosing a certain activity or path. It often made her question the extent to which individuals have unconditional responsibility and the extent to which one's influence could be exerted on others. She was merely a tiny grain of sand within the colossal beach of creation. She was a speck of dust, yet also a glistening segment of light within the entire universe's fabrication. Whilst external forces often dictated her current circumstances, ultimately, she possessed control over her feelings within those present circumstances. People may have been conditioned towards reacting in a certain way whenever their dreams or ambitions collapsed, but no one could ever force someone to *feel* something in a certain way.

Samira strongly believed that we were all victims of our current circumstances regardless of our abilities, socio-economic backgrounds, class, personalities, or any other classified figment of our imagination that we decided to use to categorise people. She believed that, ultimately, suffering was an inevitable part of the human experience above everything else. It was the one thing that was inescapable that we equally were bound to endure. Because of that, we can never be defined by our restraints but rather by the quality of our actions. It was not our physical identities or differences that limited us but rather our inability to fully love. Samira was tired of playing the blame game. Yes, the odds were always stacked against her; she could not easily obtain what she desired. But then again, whoever could? And who could fully deserve and attain their just reward without bitter struggle? She knew that, in the end, love transcended against all the odds. That will always be a universal aspect of humanity. Solely, the ability to love and to curb all limitations through love.

Chapter 9

Florence and Samira continued staring into the distance, with Samira residing next to Florence again. The sky had become significantly darker as it was around eight p.m., but they remained relaxed within their present positions.

'What were you thinking about?' Florence asked.

Samira smiled thinly whilst wriggling her toes. She somewhat enjoyed the newfound sensations within all the limbs of her body. It was almost as if she had been gifted with wings to feel more immersed within the wondrous treasures of the land surrounding her.

'Just about how I long to roam this earth freely, but that would be far too easy.'

'A girl can dream.' Florence laughed, with her glinting hazel eyes refracting tiny circles of light.

As soon as those words were released out of her mouth, she began coughing incessantly, wheezing, and inhaling whilst holding onto her chest for extra support, as though she was desperately climbing onto a lifeboat, avoiding death by drowning. As soon as clean air re-entered her lungs and her heart rate had settled, she meekly sat onto the log, regained her balance and relaxed, whilst casually brushing her hands against her lap, acting as though nothing had happened at all.

Samira observed her in disbelief. 'What's wrong? Are

you OK?'

Florence looked towards her and smiled gently. 'Actually, I have severe asthma. I crushed my inhaler, but I'll be OK.' Florence seemed totally unfazed by the fact that she was potentially further harming her health.

'Are you sure you don't want to see a doctor or something to help with that?' Samira was trying to play "The Redeemer" type of friend, attempting to resolve Florence's problems as a means of distracting herself from her own issues. As someone who had closely been affiliated with medical attention throughout most of her life, she knew that doctors could work miracles, often defeating all the odds throughout critical, unprecedented circumstances.

Florence sighed with a mixture of frustration and dismissal. 'Look, I know what I'm doing, OK? I don't need help from you. Besides, you've clearly got your medical problems sorted out already.'

Samira flinched slightly at Florence's veiled verbal attack. 'That wasn't necessary…' she whispered.

Florence looked at her incredulously again. 'Wow, you certainly are a complex individual, I'll give you that! You claim that you are super strong and in control, but really any word or phrase could shatter you at any instant. It doesn't take so much energy to crush you, isn't that right?! You're probably tearing yourself up inside right now, quivering at the thought of what icy, inhumane comment I'm going to make next! I can't believe you!'

Samira shut her eyes, attempting not to allow herself to be further wounded by Florence's overbearing misery projecting itself onto her. She had encountered people utilising Florence's defence mechanism of displacement before. Those who were unable to handle others diminishing their own value and level of confidence would rather brutally batter the self-esteem of their foes first, as a self-defence tactic, before others could gain a chance at stabbing them. It was a tale as old of time. The origin of feuds.

But Samira had grown tired of dealing with other people's drama and being dragged into it without a choice to weave herself out of it. She was often entangled in a web of lies, gossip and falsifiable rumours, all often at the expense of other's entertainment. People often thrived and exalted at witnessing others' humiliation, yet they were simultaneously too afraid to handle the humiliation and shame themselves, so they'd use their money or their previous credentials and accolades as a security blanket. Power and pride will always remain the killers of humankind, the model devices of our own hamartia. Hence, Samira was over it.

Chapter 10

Samira continued trudging along, mumbling, 'It's getting rather late, and I must continue my mission.' With the brashness of her voice being accentuated as she mentioned the word *"mission"*. She would have said more, but she decided to lock up all her thoughts firmly within her boxed mindset. Florence had once gained access to the key towards unlocking her internal mindset, her emotionally sensitive side, an element of her personality that she would rarely allow anyone to witness. But Florence had lost that offer. Samira lacked patience and overall tolerance towards offering second chances and the possibility of granting more. Particularly after understanding the minimal chance of success granted towards people utilising their empty promises.

Staring despondently in silence behind her, Florence whipped out a lighter and cigarette and began to take a puff. As she smoked, she began to ponder harder, plunging herself further and further into a whirlpool of thoughts, reflecting upon all her life decisions, her past mistakes, her wavered decisions, her errors of judgment and times where her lapse of judgment was showcased. As she exhaled, she couldn't help but feel as though Samira may not necessarily be the answer but perhaps represented a composite part of the fuel required to drive Florence back onto the right track. However, she was unsure about what exactly that path was. And now there she was, about to lose Samira. She was left with no choice but to run after her. She may not exactly believe that the medical advances and new scientific discoveries providing a formula towards the cure for her rare immune disorder (autoimmune pulmonary alveolar proteinosis) rendered as the solution towards solving her problems, but perhaps initiating a friendship may be the only thing towards guaranteeing and reaffirming her survival. She threw her cigarette over her shoulders and jogged after Samira, calling out her name.

Eventually, Florence caught up with her and tapped her lightly on the shoulder.

'You know what, I let down some of my walls for you. I know we've never met before, but I can just tell that you are ultimately a good person. I need you.'

Samira's eyes met Florence's as she looked rather bewildered, but Samira ignored this. Instead, she frowned in subtle disgust and continued walking. 'And why should I trust you?'

Florence began walking alongside her. 'There is no reason why you should. But to be frank with you, I'm a complete mess. I had so much potential in my life; I could have stood up against the bureaucratic system that I remained a part of for such a long time, but I wasted that opportunity. Not only did I waste that opportunity, but I let my emotions get the better of me and sacrificed all my life, dignity, friendships, and individuality as a result. I'm a lost cause, Samira. I may look perfect to you or anyone else. But I'm just a withered flower, waiting for my petals to dry up and disperse into the surroundings. I know that you're on a mission right now to find the Sphere of Restrictions or whatever to cease the calamity and impending extinction of humankind, but I honestly don't know how much time is left for me. And I don't want to seek medical assistance. I need something more. I don't know exactly what it is, but whatever it is that you're searching for… I'm willing to find it also.'

'*No,*' Samira stated.

Florence felt her heart stop beating for a second. '*What do you mean, no?*'

'I didn't mean it in that context. I meant to apologise. This is my wrongdoing. I treated you in the same way that individuals had treated me throughout my entire life. I disregarded you. I turned away from you, even though I could clearly observe your internal battle. I left you in the dark.

'I'm sorry if I seem arrogant, conceited or too self-absorbed to you. I am completely unaware sometimes of how cold and blunt I may appear towards others. I judged you before understanding you first. But I have been taught not to judge others from first glance, particularly when I have never seen them exhibit any wrongdoing. I was intimidated by you. I believed that you were too self-assured and proud. I was afraid of being hurt, even though I thought that I was OK with dealing with the possibility of pain, but no matter the level of intensity or proximity, that pain is bound to hurt you; either way, it somehow always will. You're right; I am a complex, contradictory human being. We all are. We all strive to desperately achieve what we want or what we believe that we need. In spite of this, we fail to acknowledge the fact that our achievements are ephemeral; only our bitterness endures. But we found each other for a reason. And like you, I do not see the point of wasting an opportunity. That would only harm me tomorrow and for the rest of my days to come.'

'I accept your apology, and I hope that you are willing to accept mine.'

'Always. I can promise you that.'

'Then consider our covenant sealed,' Florence exclaimed with reverence. 'Although, I may need to use you as a guide… I destroyed my spectacles, and my vision is rather poor. I used to wear contact lenses, but I did not want to remain a part of or become an object of the material world. I just found it all so unconventional.'

'Why did you destroy your glasses?' Samira questioned bluntly.

'Oh, so is this an interrogation now? Never mind, I'm joking. I was just tired of looking at everything with clarity. I experienced an epiphany after fleeing from the asylum, and I realised that our entire civilisation was a formulation of concocted lies and lost disfigured ideals. I was so tired of observing all the destruction within our world. It's rationally nonsensical! The darkness, the ceasefires, the physical abuse in the streets… I was entangled within a maze of excruciating pain, broken visions, collapsed masterpieces and fallen landmarks of grandeur. Everything instead had become digitalised, without any real means of contact or connection. I am unable to even drive my own car as I need tactile identification, instead of physical keys to unlock the vehicle, as everything is automated! It's almost as though we are literally losing ourselves to determinism. Suddenly, our free will, the greatest gift offered to mankind besides unconditional love, has been eroded by our own corporate greed and sloth. We have enslaved ourselves with nonsensical deceit. Therefore, I'd rather become totally blind as a means of escaping this imperious nightmare.'

Samira's heart rate began racing rapidly as a result of Florence's vented frustration. Samira felt comforted by the fact that she was not the only one dissatisfied with the modern world but simultaneously grew anxious at the potential thought of failing her mission. But she relied upon Florence to serve as a form of distraction. Her own troubles could wait.

'You know, I used to have incredibly poor vision too... I thought that suddenly "healing" from my visual impairments would feel satisfying and empowering, but it is only causing me to feel further dejected by the world's problems and the prevalent injustice. Before you stopped wearing your glasses, did you see a group of Arabian men running?'

'Oh yes, they have been around here for quite a while. They've been ordered by the government to destroy places of worship or solitude.'

'Why is that the case?'

'Because the government believes that those organisations possess "unprofitable" value.'

'This makes no sense...' Samira struggled to remain

stable after discovering those foreboding circumstances, epitomising further termination of the general tranquillity embedded within the core of the Natural World.

Ever since the Second Wave of Destruction, (a sudden pandemic which had wiped out more than fifty per cent of the entire human population at an equal proportion across every continent and island), all jurisdictions, constitutions and governmental organisations gradually resigned their power over the course of hundred years and instead combined all authority to create the One World Government, a totalitarian government that functioned predominantly on capitalist ideals, which was largely accepted by people of all cultures after recovering from a major economic recession. The One World Government comprised of executive, legislative and judicial functions, all working together in an administrative fashion, yet it was ultimately facilitated by technological influences. In essence, these devices dictated the educational system, various corporate businesses, medical surgeries and commercialised brands whilst eradicating manual labour and domestic activities, including cooking and cleaning, as there are special tools doing all the work. Everyone attended meetings remotely with interactive features and all-important achievements, news and profiles of every citizen would be displayed on a universal webpage, which anyone could possibly access without difficulty.

Regardless, approximately a year ago, an extremist group, predominantly comprised of religious fanatics known as the "Zellites", revolted and rebelled, intending to eradicate technology. This led towards the various presidents of the One World Government ordering many places of religious worship or quiet areas to be demolished until further notice, attempting to silence the Zellites. The Zellites sought hiding as a result, but shortly afterwards, more earthquakes, typhoons and natural disasters worldwide occurred, which many people named "Natural Punishment" as they believed that the natural law had been disobeyed. However, there was a lack of proof attached to that theory and since then, many people feared that eternal deformation would occur, which increased the amount of tension and paranoia displayed within the society, which consisted of both elements of Eastern and Western ideals.

However, Samira was unaware of the political circumstances around society as she had been in hiding with the Sage for several months after her neighbours, The Senators, threatened to send her to prison after she was framed for murdering their Border Terrier. At the time, Samira was infuriated by the level of injustice and was ostracised by the most influential people in her suburban neighbourhood. She even feared going to the grocery store to buy milk as any action that she made could easily be used against her, fabricated as further evidence towards her neighbours' reprobate case, much to her dismay.

'Yes, anyway, considering the fact that it is quite late now, I believe that it would be best for us to seek refuge in a safe haven temporarily.'

'So be it,' Samira mumbled bleakly.

The two continued walking in silence, growing more fatigued, until they found a medium-sized hut in the corner of a field, surrounded by several oak trees. The sky was pitch black, with a few stars dotted above, shining with a rather dim light, as the wind grew chillier, drawing an end to Florence and Samira's tiring day after previously absorbing the summer heat for several hours.

Chapter 11

It was eleven a.m. The sun remained hidden behind several thin sheets of grey clouds, permeating the subtle cyan-blue hue of the sky above. The atmosphere remained pleasantly calm with near silence, besides tree branches bristling amidst the gentle heat and a few blackbirds waddling alongside the meadow below. Samira and Florence had sought shelter and caught up on sleep on the wooden floors after instantly gaining access to a hut, which had an open door and was astoundingly empty. The two young adults were unaware of the identity of the true owner of the property upon which they had trespassed, but they refused to take much acknowledgement of it regardless.

Within their gaze as they both opened their eyes, absorbing their surroundings within the late morning light, they realised that the hut was larger than they had initially perceived and there were stacks of pews arranged almost symmetrically on both sides with an aisle split vertically down the middle of the room, and an altar in the centre-front, resembling the design of a traditional church. Both girls blinked in fervent disbelief.

'I don't understand,' Florence stammered, 'I thought that this was a mellow hut…'

'Well, things don't always appear to be exactly what we believe them to be at first glance,' Samira responded bluntly.

'Huh? This is insane!' Florence continued to remain astounded by the physical surroundings. They both continued to accustom themselves towards the unfamiliarity of the building they found themselves placed in and continued to wander around wistfully. Florence began to cough irreverently again, bellowing for pure oxygen at the sole of her lungs. She clutched her chest and tried to compose herself by inhaling slowly and gently until the chest pain was slightly less severe. She felt a deep aching swelling within her chest, which would only become tighter and heavier as more mucus and toxins congested her inner lungs, further corrupting her respiratory system.

'I'm going to go outside for some fresh air for a little bit and to take a puff.' Her eyes lit up in subtle anticipation and a burst of excitement as she quickly dashed off and left the building.

Samira stared at the door in mild shock, slightly startled. She was amazed at Florence's adamance towards seeking medical assistance despite her health remaining in a rather detrimental state. Moreover, her preferences and personal inclinations which mainly involved resorting towards unhealthy habits with confidence were even more astonishing. Samira was slightly envious of Florence's ability to remain calm, composed and content despite the disconcerting circumstances facing her. This included the never-ending uncertainty, instability, symptoms of loss and despondent concerns appearing out of nowhere in addition to fear of what is seen and unknown alongside conflict of all sizes, shapes and forms. These were issues which constantly swirled and lingered around Samira's mind. Likewise, she recognised Florence's awareness and present anxiety surrounding these issues too. But for some reason, they were irrelevant to her. But then again, Samira had only just met the girl, and it was clear that she had already coped with enough issues in her life already, with relative success.

But what mostly captivated Samira at that moment was the altar design. It glimmered with exceptional simplicity, depicting a dainty white sheet covering the broad, rectangular and rather sturdy wooden table.

Samira was well aware of the fact that the altar signified a place of sacrifice, a place of reverence, a source of redemption where all our laboured burdens could rest. It epitomised the one point of time where no harm could be done, where a miracle could possibly take place. The Sage had once reminded her that the altar was like a pit stop for *"penitent worriers that longed for grace"*. Samira was unsure about whether she could align herself the established definition for penitent worrier or what the suitable requirements to meet the criteria of a *"penitent worrier"* resembled. But regardless of her worldview, she needed guidance at this moment. She needed to find and rest upon a pillar of certainty to carry her tightly through and across the unstable tide of perturbed clamour, which was forged within the depths of her imagination, gradually drifting herself away as a further descent of her own madness. She needed to decrease the temperature of her heated mindset. Hence, she profoundly desired to find something uplifting, especially as she had no crystallised perception or signal displaying her true fate.

'Please,' she whispered, 'help me in my mission... help me to find the right way so that I may know the truth and safeguard my life...'

She continued sighing and whispering pensively and silently lowered her head attentively, with transfixed concentration, remaining mesmerised yet grounded at the same time.

Until Florence burst into the building again, her face beaming with excitement as her pupils dilated, like an excited child overloaded with energy after receiving their favourite gift, which they had desperately longed for.

'Samira! I found someone who could help us to find the Sphere of Restrictions! He's a theologian turned mad scientist named Thomas!'

'As in doubting Thomas?' Samira questioned in a hushed tone.

'No, just Thomas! Come, you need to meet him!' Florence ran up to Samira and grabbed hold of her wrist firmly, urging her to follow her. Samira quickly turned towards the altar again, looked at it again with melancholic sorrow and slight adoration, gently bowed her head again towards it and turned away, exiting the building alongside Florence.

Chapter 12

The two girls were standing once again in the meadow. But as Samira shifted her eyes towards the left, she noticed a tall man with a towering presence leaning casually against one of the thick oak trees in the background. He appeared to be in his mid-thirties and had brunette unkempt hair alongside a bristly beard which spiked outwards, accompanying his scruffy exterior style. He wore a long brown T-shirt, covered in specks of thick dust, as if he had spent hours working on carpentry, as well as long dark trousers resembling an earth-like shade, covering the tips of his shoes. He caught Samira's gaze for a second and then swiftly sprung out a Pink Lady Apple from his pocket and chomped vociferously whilst devouring its scrumptious taste. As he continued biting the apple, he began to scratch his beard, unfazed by the girls' reaction to him. He seemed to exude a totally relaxed yet meandered outlook, as though he was used to people casually observing him and posing their own judgments. Yet, he remained unaffected by any sort of active reaction which would pressure him towards changing his demeanour, to perhaps try to appear more presentable...

Florence smiled awkwardly and introduced Samira to the strange man. 'Samira, this is Thomas! He's offered to help us discover where the Sphere of Restrictions is located as he is aware of its relevant history.'

Thomas took a few steps forward and glanced curiously at Samira, inspecting her thoroughly as if she were an undiscovered object capable of shifting the motion of time or the order of the Natural World. 'Actually, it's TO-MARSS.'

Samira looked up at him, slightly stunned by his thick Greek accent. Samira quickly realised that it was best not to judge a book by its cover and tried to remain polite upon greeting him, extending her right hand. 'I'm Samira,' she whispered meekly.

'Hmmm… you are from the evening conversationalist?'

'Yes, that's right,' Samira responded, remaining rather cautious of Tomas' rather obvious dialectical inefficiencies. He was not the first she had encountered of someone struggling to communicate coherently and clearly in expressed English. She was aware that English was possibly the most preferable language to speak universally and was rather popular amongst the entire population, which was further instilled by the influence of the Commonwealth and previous colonisation, including the original colonisation of the thirteen colonies in the United States. But she also recognised the common difficulty within reading, writing, listening and speaking to someone in English or in any other predominant language almost perfectly from scratch. Not everyone was competent linguistically. Likewise, not everyone was particularly gifted in mathematics or the creative arts. Nevertheless, she accepted the fact that learning a language was an incredibly effective skill and a way to become more immersed in a different culture rather than being restricted by the geographical barriers imposed across the planet.

Moreover, Samira also recognised how people were often further divided by their ineptitude and ostracisation towards understanding different cultures. Xenophobia was particularly targeted towards Eastern areas, yet it could also be rather prevalent within one specific and supposedly *"unified"* country with multiple personalities, multiple interests, traditions, and cultural conceptions combined into one. Versatility and diversity were strengths regarded as the essence of humanity, capable of enhancing a different way of functioning and automatically granting new insights. Yet, our hesitance towards implementing social change, especially after recognising admissible achievements demonstrated by specific cultures (which was usually further ingrained within traditional practices or narrow-minded emic perspectives), often provided a significant barrier towards acknowledging areas of development to initiate further progress. Hence, fervent resistance leads towards the perpetuation of inferiority to the superiority of a specific class, which was widely and subconsciously accepted as a means of asserting inadequate subjugation.

What saddened Samira the most was the fact that those regarded as ultimately inferior (often the minorities in this subconscious battle) were usually those who were dismissed and those who would continue to struggle, left in the shadows, merely because they were branded by society as failing to reach acceptable standards of class and social etiquette. Within the modern world, sophistication embedded in bureaucracy was regarded as a necessity for those who longed to remain wealthy and successful. That was an unfortunate truth which was rather stagnant and unlikely to change.

'Ah, so I see it. And yes, yet you are seeking a sphere of restrictions?' Tomas asked.

Samira simply nodded her head. She generally disliked small talk and she felt as though it was unnecessary to overwhelm Thomas with her many thoughts. She wondered how extraverts felt so comfortable saying whatever they felt at the top of their heads without any form or possibility of apprehension occurring, which could perhaps make the situation more awkward. Sometimes, Samira longed for it to be possible for her also to casually engage in a conversation and to feel a sense of joy and ecstasy from it rather than constantly overthinking her every word for fear of further judgment or discrimination. She was often frustrated about how selectively mute individuals like her were often encouraged to speak up and yet the consequence of that would usually be ridicule. She remained baffled at how many confident people failed to understand that.

Florence jumped into the conversation abruptly. 'Yes, and you were telling me before, Tomas, about where it is located and how to get there?' as she reassured Tomas, her eyes sparkled again; it was clear that new knowledge was something that instantly excited her, almost consisting of a type of distraction from all the past decisions and regrets that she had made recently within her own life.

Tomas hesitated for a bit and then lifted his eyebrows in agreement. 'Yes, I will show you its map.'

Samira then leaned in slightly, stating, 'Actually, before you do so... I was wondering if Florence and I could eat something quickly beforehand as we are rather hungry at the moment?' Samira and Florence had been snacking on Florence's stash of Twix bars, which she had kept in her satchel for the past forty-eight hours. Samira, on the other hand, had begun her journey empty-handed and remained empty-handed without food or water, so she desperately needed to stock up as she did not intend to take trips to the grocery store with the little amount of currency that she possessed.

Tomas looked slightly dazzled for a second and then quickly nodded his head and ran his hands through his hair with a rather flushed expression. 'Yes, but of course, I will show you what I eat to you.'

The two girls then followed Tomas towards another smaller room a few metres behind the little hut that they had previously entered, walking silently yet feeling slightly more settled than before, aware that they were making greater progress within their quest.

Chapter 13

A gentle breeze arose within the atmosphere as the sun reached its peak within the boundless, kaleidoscopic landscape stretching vastly across the blue skies above. Florence, Samira, and Tomas meekly entered the little room beside the tiny hut, and sat on tiny wooden stools, forming a minuscule circle. They gathered together as if they were conducting a regular ritual. Tomas picked up a few loaves of bread stored on the side cabinets and offered pieces to the young girls, who quickly accepted his offer, chewing peacefully and consuming every little crumb whilst sipping on glasses of water to aid their digestive systems.

'So,' Florence stated, attempting to break the awkward silence between them all, 'how do we find the Sphere of Restrictions, Tomas?'

Tomas looked at her for a second, hung his head down, frowned as his brow furrowed, looked up again, maintaining eye contact with her every few or so seconds and then looking at the ground again with a rather solemn expression.

'You have seen, the Sphere of Restrictions is not such an object but, in fact, of vortex type.'

'What do you mean?' Florence asked as Samira continued eating her loaf of bread in silence but listened thoroughly and intently.

'The Sphere come to you; it is not where you go… Legend has foretold that it will come to a hour of peril need…'

'So, you're telling me that it is not actually an object but rather a random place that magically appears to us during a time of serious danger and has no specific location?'

'Yes.' Tomas nodded meekly in approval.

'Great! That solves all my life's problems!' Florence admitted sarcastically, raising her hands up in frustration and slouching back whilst sagging her shoulders as she sank further down into her stool.

'No, no, there is no need for us to renounce ourselves and to lose our determination and overall willpower towards continuing our journey. There is still a possible chance that the Sphere will reach us in time,' Samira whispered, mildly surprised at her sudden optimistic approach.

'See, see, she has reason…' Tomas' eyes sparkled slightly after previously appearing rather dim and deflated. 'There is a chance; no one knows when it is to be coming, but it will be here when you need it. You must open your eyes to see it!'

'Open my eyes? Open my eyes and then a random vortex thing will pop into my vision, out of nowhere?! Please, I don't need any sort of make-believe nonsense; I don't trust this hypothesis for a second. I have standards, but these standards lack any rational explanation! Call me a sceptic if you must, but you simply CANNOT expect me to just continue walking and wasting my life, hoping for some vortex to come around and magically dissolve all conflicts and possible further threats towards humanity's existence. It's totally unreasonable. It's simply absurd!'

Florence had now stood up, her face reddening with a mixture of fury and frustration, highly bent on dismissing any possible stance of optimism which posed itself as a significant obstacle towards providing her with any sanity at that given moment. She was fed up with just waiting; she wanted to figure out all the possible solutions herself. For her, when life lacked true meaning, she always believed that it was right to create some sort of purpose or goal for herself personally, out of any meaningless, meagre existence, as a means of bringing a sense of control within the tumultuous chaos of her own existence, where others often dictated her actions for her. She was often silenced because she was deemed too young and too inexperienced. She had never really grasped an opportunity to complete a project herself within an impoverished state, with a lack of resources or constant guidance surrounding her. She believed that she owed it to herself to create a greater self-assured purpose for herself, to self-actualise her full, complete potential through finding the Sphere. And yet, again, she was only obliged to remain passive. A tendency that she had become accustomed to throughout her entire life.

'I am sorry, there are no means to upset you...' Tomas stammered in fright in response to Florence's apparent *meltdown*.

Florence coughed suddenly and began to walk out.

'Sorry, I need some air…'

Samira also got up, sympathising with her friend. 'Actually, I need to go too… Thanks for your help, Tomas.' She gave him a reassuring smile and quickly followed Florence.

Tomas smiled back. 'You are most of welcome.'

Chapter 14

Florence stormed off and failed to console herself outside, panting and sighing in exasperation.

'Can you believe that guy? The nerve... He said that some vortex is magically going to appear out of somewhere. That's never going to happen.'

'At least we're fed.'

'We're fed? You know what? If anything, I'm still hungry for knowledge!'

'But that's dangerous. Plunging ourselves further into the sea of knowledge, wealth, power, and prosperity often only leads towards greater detrimental circumstances for humankind. Gathering more knowledge is unnecessary for satiating our thirst; it will only hinder our progress.'

'No, you're dangerous! Every single word that comes out of your mouth is a pure measure of your own insanity! Don't bother fooling yourself, believing that you will be able to indoctrinate me with your nonsensical belief system because, trust me, you have no chance!'

Samira stared in austere disbelief at Florence's childish pettiness, which was comprised of heavy frustration in conjunction with unbridled angst. She was acting as though the two had failed a simple mission. Samira, however, remained stern and refused to allow Florence's wave of fury to wash over her, simultaneously drowning within her own tears of sorrow. If anything, that would make their whole situation even more futile, and Samira, within her newfound state, was unwilling to surrender so soon.

Florence wheezed for a second and rapidly blinked with tears flowing down her cheeks whilst doing so. 'Forgive me, Samira, I am sorry. I don't deserve your respect or utmost attention. I don't even trust myself. I don't deserve anything. I'm a complete mess. I can't even last for five minutes without throwing myself into a coughing fit.'

Samira continued staring at Florence for a couple of seconds, unsure about how to offer reassurance during her pitiful hour of need. Regardless, after much deliberation, she mustered enough compassion to offer Florence an affectionate smile despite the clear pain prevailing within her eyes. As a former paraplegic, Samira had been conditioned with the belief that she deserved the most pity for her condition. Yet, time and time again, she'd encounter many broken individuals occasionally, ranging from those who were able-bodied, to those who handled critical, terminal conditions or those coping with severe grief, with internalised wounds. She realised that no matter how carefree one would appear at the outset, often they would have to cope with minimal or major shortcomings. Suffering was indeed inevitable for everyone, and Florence was a clear example disproving the fact that money, wealth, status, or one's level of attraction within a superficial environment and privilege would ultimately provide happiness. Money may make the world go round, but it can never remove suffering from the earth's innermost core. It could never rewind time, either. No matter what source or accomplishment humanity could possibly initiate, pain would always persist.

'Also, I must confess... I apologise for not being completely honest with you, but I don't have severe asthma. In fact, I have a rare autoimmune condition disorder thing known as autoimmune pulmonary alveolar proteinosis. That's why I keep coughing. I was hoping that locating the Sphere of Restrictions would provide some kind of solution for me or even a remnant of hope. But apparently, that's not the case...' Florence stumbled on some of her words, allowing emotion to convey her debilitating state as her tears continued to glisten upon her dainty white cheeks, retaining a light shade of pink planted upon her freckled skin.

'I am sorry. After all, there is still time,' Samira reluctantly admitted she was not exactly content with providing false hope.

'Time? You know what? Time is exactly the issue here. Samira, I don't know how much time I have left. That's often the case when you're coping with a serious diagnosis, and you're just forced to continue living, dealing with the anguish and constant apprehension surrounding the fact that we will never know for sure when the clock is going to stop chiming! That's the ultimate limit.

'I'm sorry; I just feel as though I have waited my whole life for some kind of miraculous cure to turn up or for a little glimpse of my symptoms easing so I will no longer have to struggle with this unbearable pain. But I feel as though no matter the circumstances or potential chances of recovery; I'm always going to be waiting and hoping, without any means of reaching a sufficient end, where I feel truly satisfied or content with my condition. Despite trying or praying even, it all amounts to nothing. I just feel like a complete mess. I'm nothing more than a failure. How can there ever be any sort of value towards our circumstances of living when we are obligated to just cope and continue despite all the odds being stacked against us? I see no chance of improvement. I just want it all to stop forever.'

Samira's stare gradually grew more distant as she fixated her vision on a valley in the background.

'I see your point, Florence,' she admitted bluntly.

'It is rational to despair. It is rational enough for us to foresee death as the ultimate forthcoming relief of all unbearable suffering, despite a lack of clarity over what is to come… But the way I see it is that, in some way, there is a truth conveyed within, knowing that we receive no particular gain from death. Death renders itself as a total elimination of choice. It merely consists of ultimate anguish towards those that we have left behind. It solely comprises of an eternalised censure that one could never return from. Death is what equally deprives us of everything, regardless of our origins.

Yet, what we fear most regarding death is its irreversible effect. At least, within our lifetimes, endless possibilities for growth, renewal, and renovation remain. Change is always certain. Death, on the other hand, removes this possibility of certainty. Within death, there is no chance of change. That's the predominant reason for why I see life as worthwhile, withstanding all the odds. The opportunity for transformation always holds greater significance…'

'Yes, I see that now.' Florence snapped, abruptly interrupting Samira's train of thought within that moment, intentionally. 'That's easy for you to say! You have suddenly been *healed* from your tone-deaf, blind paraplegic state. You have absolutely NOTHING to worry about. But I'm standing right here as my life is slowly fading. As if everything could not possibly become worse. Tell me, what exactly is there for me to hope for? My family are ashamed of me; my friends resent me for escaping from that burdensome lifestyle. I currently have a low supply of oxygen without any possible remedy! I don't see any beauty or single reminiscence of hope protruding from this circumstance. You may as well allow me to be alone!'

'No, I cannot leave you here, Florence! You don't deserve to suffer alone.'

'Wow, now I've got you pitying me. Don't bother sticking around, Samira; it will only become worse at this rate.'

Samira looked down towards the ground and shifted her feet a bit, trying desperately not to appear uncomfortable with Florence's outbursts.

'You know, I've always felt out of place. The thing is, I never bothered to belong. I always believed that society would never accept me. But then again, society never really accepts anyone. Often, we're faced with circumstances where we're expected to fully express ourselves and to feel comfortable with knowing who we truly are whilst always encouraging others to become their authentic selves. We're constantly faced with expectations that we're meant to meet and as soon as we fall short of those expectations, we're instantly disregarded. Because of our unhealthy appearances or behaviour, we fail to belong. We're considered as unattractive. But even whilst standing here in my current "healthy" form, a prominent aspect continues to remain. The fact that I must constantly act desirable, second-guessing every decision that I feel entitled to make, in fear of disappointing others. Despite it all, the prospect of failing to meet those standards and confronting truly humiliating circumstances remains. Within life, there always remains a possibility that I am trapped and only defined by others' expectations of me. I constantly must deal with the fact that my worth only exists within the eyes of others.' Knowing that my own estimate of my worth and potential will *never* be enough.'

Florence sat down on a kerb of the nearby road that the two were walking towards, both unsure of where they were really headed, yet plodding onwards regardless. Samira looked at her, hesitating slightly, but then sat opposite her, sitting on the edge of the road. Florence gave a heavy sigh and looked straight into Samira's eyes, upholding an austere glance.

'Believe it or not, I can relate… When I was younger, I was desperate to seek everyone's approval. I wanted to appear self-assured and respectable in the eyes of my elders so that they would withhold themselves from scolding me or dismissing me entirely. I believed that partying constantly with my friends, binge drinking and the like would advance me into a classy socialite. But in the end, I became so miserable. I lost a sense of not only who I was as a person but also losing sight of my true, valid intentions. I wanted to be loved by everyone but struggled to find a reason to love and respect myself. I believed that dressing up in expensive, lavish jewellery and gowns would enhance my social status and increase my general amicability, but it never did. Instead, I became increasingly moodier, withdrawing myself from my friends and everyone, trying to brush everything off independently until one day, I just lost it. I ran off, smashed glass windows, committed theft, and became imprisoned in a mental asylum. Society would label me as an insane criminal; I'd label myself as a crestfallen soul. The thing is that I never meant to harm anyone, but the pressure that others imposed upon me just escalated towards a level that was unbearable, and no one was on my side. I was tired of facing it alone, so I acted out. I suppressed who I really was, concealed my true nature and struggles with illness and the like to blend in, to appear appealing. Sometimes, I wondered what was the point, why did I always need to act to feel accepted. But then again, I realised that my options were rather scarce. But in reality, appearances amount to nothing. It all means nothing. Besides, we only have one judge, the Creator... What would they think of me now?

I'm sorry, but I just cannot fixate myself on the idea or speculation of an unknown higher power readily capable of redeeming me from my own shortcomings. Are we all destined to become punished and further corrupted for our endless deceit? Why must there be any complications?'

Florence was growing increasingly frustrated as Samira observed quietly, unsure about how to react or what to think. She was captivated mostly by Florence's questions, questions which could be extended towards all of humanity. Possible chances of redemption were essential at this point, but were they ever truly guaranteed? The problem of evil and natural suffering was an issue which constantly swirled and embedded itself within Samira's mind. Often, it would challenge her own sanity, leading towards herself internally battling harsh criticism. Believing that she was typically deserving of suffering as it was truly inevitable for her. Facing life, the hard way, as such, was an ominous truth that comprised her foundation. Yet, at the same time, she wondered to what extent these harsh circumstances would culminate towards her Final Fate. She would question how much more difficult life needed to be for her before falling at the final hurdle. However, she realised that pondering on these issues would only demotivate her from pursuing her own happiness and attaining genuine freedom, remaining even more frozen within her formerly immobile state.

'No, you are right. Life will never be just. But losing our own sense of integrity and shifting the blame will only make our struggles more unbearable. Pondering upon our potential survival is insignificant. Instead, we must confront and accept all that remains here within ourselves today.'

Florence's eyes gradually regained the initial curious

spark that was initially present during her first meeting with Samira. Her demeanour relaxed a bit, and she began to stand up.

'I know... I just needed to hear that from someone else.' She looked down towards Samira and smiled, extending her hand to pull her up from the ground, which was lightly dusted as streams of sunlight glistened behind her, warming their surroundings, similarly to how Samira's optimism was transferring itself onto Florence.

Samira maintained eye contact with her and smiled warmly, sharing an embrace with her.

'HALT!' a loud voice yelled in the background as the girls turned their heads and noticed a swarm of soldiers pointing at the girls and running vociferously towards them, disrupting their reconciliation. Before the girls could anticipate any further action, the soldiers ran up to where they were standing and whipped out a can with some sort of sedative gas, knocking them out instantly as they became unconscious and thudded onto the ground.

Chapter 15

Florence

Florence awoke within a cell. It was vacant and dark, without a window or any form of light seeping through. The atmosphere was entirely dormant, tight, and miniscule. There was barely enough room to stand, as she was rendered without even a mattress accompanying her. She rapidly moved her head around, incredulously surveying her surroundings as her teal blue eyes widened, conveying a mixture of terror and petrification, with a hint of despondence and understandable irritation.

'Who do you people think you are? Get me out of here!' she bellowed from the depths of her lungs, as her voice carried over echoing. She mumbled expletives under her breath and trudged backwards, supporting her back against the cold, stony wall behind her, exhaling, coughing, and sighing. As her rage culminated inside her, she remained still, adamantly refusing to believe that her most intense anxieties were attacking her. Once again, she was faced with something equivalent to her most profound torment, her own personal oblivion, narrowly restraining her.

Samira

Samira tensed up as all the colour illuminating from the pallor of her dark skin faded and changed into grey. Despite being capable of feeling multiple sensations that were previously unknown to her, they had been replaced by pure numbness. Every inkling of colour had disappeared within her system. Every particle consuming the internal network of her nervous system with energy and sparks, converting themselves into life, derived from different streams of passion ranging from mild to moderate to extreme, had withered. She was suddenly left with nothing. She had become nothing.

She tried to move, she tried to stand up, but her immense heartache was burying and pinning her stiff body against the surface. Time had been replaced and surpassed by sentiments of woe. Everything surrounding her consisted of nullity. She didn't even want to question why she was captured. All that was certain was the fact that she was trapped within the present moment, only completely immobile. Any thoughts correlating with optimism or change were futile. She lacked the energy to speak, to move, to even think about something positive.

Instead, her mind wandered to a time when she was in class with an able-bodied student as well as a deaf boy and another girl with selective mutism. She would try to walk with her prosthetic legs whilst the other comrades within her class were playing games. Often, Samira was unable to participate in these games as she was naturally hindered by her condition. As she was attempting to walk around the playground on her own within her own space, a teacher approached her.

'You child,' the teacher said to her, maintaining a stern, austere expression with an icy, sycophantic tone within his voice, narrowing his eyes down at her whilst simultaneously frowning in disgust.

'Yes, sir,' a young Samira whispered, struggling to locate and meet his gaze whilst adjusting her hearing aids.

'You are wasting your time, attempting to walk around. You should not even be entitled to become a part of this school. You are a disgrace to our system. Other children, such as Jacinta and Frances, are thriving around here. Lucio may be hard of hearing, but at least he is capable of helping out and maintaining his demeanour as a good citizen within our community. But you will always need to be aided and supported. For what good do you possibly have to offer this world? Within your lifetime, everything that you do will be restricted. You are never going to be like anyone else, despite any ideas you may have, because you are purely a malfunction. I'm sure that people will barely be able to look at you straight in the eyes without a hint of sympathy or some subtle, veiled form of disdain. You will always have the bare minimum or possibly even less to prove. So, you may as well not bother.'

He confidently strode off, feeling rather satisfied with himself for spouting out his despicable outburst of the "truth", scowled at her once more and began conversing happily with another student. Samira stared at him, appalled at his behaviour and disparaging attitude towards her. She often felt out of place, but being reminded of it and spoken to as if she was an unpalatable, mouldy dirt mound trotted on and tapered while remaining idly on the ground crossed the line. Anger also swept across her face within that moment; she was tempted towards harming him back, wounding him, damaging his career and asserting her vindictive nature, but regardless, she would only be rendered more vulnerable within the circumstance. She often wondered what exactly is disrupted within the neurochemistry of one's brain, which causes them to exert such hard cruelty. And that wasn't even the least of our civilisation's most heinous acts. The fractured status of humankind often pushed Samira to withhold herself from sharing mere smithereens of benevolence towards others.

Yet again, she would fixate her mind on the Golden Rule or any other alternative source of morality and try her hardest towards actively forgetting, ignoring, and avoiding the incessant harm unleashed onto those who are facing even greater abuse, recovering from traumatic situations, rape, grief, murder, solitude, homelessness, and everything else that one can depict as totally unjustifiable. Yet, no irreparable solution would come to mind. It was entirely out of her hands.

This paralleled starkly with the situation that she now found herself in, locked up and detained against her will without a fair trial or hearing. All that remained were corrupt, indignant individuals who were incapable of showcasing any integrity, yet solely allocated deciding her own fate, despite Samira doing nothing whatsoever to harm the state or delineate the incomprehensible standards of the current criminal justice system. Instead, she was incarcerated involuntarily with no possible solution or formula available to redeem herself.

Chapter 16

Florence

Florence adjusted herself, leaning entirely onto the wall behind her, rolling her neck and attempting to relax her shoulders as a migraine pounded against her cranium. In her highly restless, agitated state, the only ideas instilled in the depths of her mind consisted principally of escaping by any means necessary.

It was almost as though her mind was a lucid whirlpool. She was so sleep-deprived and out of touch without any remnant of reality pushing her forward. Hence, it remained impossible for her to keep track of time, monitor her sanity or even to plan out her next steps.

Dealing with hypomania in any form was impossible to tame; it was almost as though bursts of energy had conjoined themselves into a little figure, rampaging around with unrestrainable and intolerable speed whilst entering Florence's body and controlling her every move, before she even had an inch of a second to carefully contemplate her next motive and activate it.

Her impulses had separated themselves from her own grasp, and rather, she was confronted with intangible ardour, capable of destroying every flicker of reason that remained within her current state of mind. She found herself instead reluctant, breathing heavily, attempting to minimise the unwavering overload of energy, overcoming her entire system. She continued panting, crashing her forehead against the wall incessantly and recklessly, whilst digging her nails into her wrists and screaming aloud, like an untamed wildebeest, losing her humanity and being ruled by passion, something which was highly disapproved by those above the bourgeois class and higher social circles that she had remained a part of throughout the majority of her life.

As her thoughts scattered elsewhere, pacing back and forth, her heartbeat elevating at an abnormal rate, amid coughing out more mucus from her system. The only possibility that remained to salvage her entire being was located within the presence of another human being, perhaps someone more compassionate, more understanding. She desperately needed to find someone who could relate to her condition in comparison to her state, where she was rendered entirely out of place.

As always, she concluded that hope was only ascertainable through patience.

As her eyelids grew heavy and sticky, resting her head onto a nearby stone pillar within her cell, Florence indulged herself in her own haven and fell heavily into a slumber, drifting unobtrusively off to sleep.

Samira

'It is finished… it is finished… why have you left me without her? Why have you left us behind? What kind of

101

benevolent creature are you?' Samira whispered to herself as she lay down on the floor, as she scarcely resisted cursing against the Creator. She was aware that it was not necessarily right or wrong for her to displace blame, but mostly, she internalised all the resentment, frustration, and disappointment onto herself. She tried to remain faithful to her ambitions. She tried to remain faithful towards herself, but now she was falling further down the verge of self-destruction without desiring or yearning for change. Instead, she only hoped for imminent external destruction, which was most likely looming at any second.

She breathed slowly, unfazed by any potential surprise or element of harm, instead berating herself for failing to try harder to release herself from this surreal version of false imprisonment as the hours rolled by.

'Samira? Samira?' Samira's eyes opened and darted around the room, once again locating where the voice's parameters were.

'I am not who you are seeking. Leave me be.'

'Samira... do not be disheartened. I am with you in spirit.' Samira recognised the Sage's voice but failed to witness any beam of light or anything resembling her pristine figure at all. Instead, she continued to rest, remaining in bleak darkness.

Florence

Florence stood still, stifled by mortifying insights and haunting lamentations of terror dominating her mindset, with the sounds of metal clanging and chiming together as her body remained frozen.

A tall, young man appearing to be in his early thirties stood before her. He had slick back hair and a tanned complexion, supposedly from a mixed background with dark hair at the roots with a mixture of chestnut-brown and dyed blonde highlights with golden blonde tips, in a cowlick style. His complexion appeared to be smooth like a wax statue and rather appealing, resembling a national treasure of art. He unlocked the chamber where Florence resided and entered the room, his sharp green eyes twinkling luminously. The room may have been rather cold at first glance, but after this mysterious hero's entrance, everything gradually began to warm up.

'Who are you?' Florence grunted, overwhelmed with fatigue and reluctant to create a charming first impression.

'My name is Antoniadis Rivieras. But feel free to call me Antonio,' Antonio beamed, showcasing a full set of straight teeth, gleaming like an intricately designed composition of gemstones, primarily diamonds and pearls. He spoke rather quickly with a sophisticated, British accent and appeared to be incredibly confident and easy-going, despite the position that Florence was currently in, leaving her bemused at how this impossibly handsome chap had endeavoured to break her free.

She looked at him, slightly intrigued but mostly displeased, extending her hand, which was beginning to feel numb. 'I'm Florence. Do you care to explain why I'm in this mess right now as well as where on earth my friend is located too?'

Antonio looked at her with an erratic, yet amused,

expression as he fell into a fit of hysterics, laughing restlessly and uncontrollably. Florence stared at him with a measured approach, desperately attempting to conceal venting as a means of coping with her ingrained rage.

'Well, Florence. You're held captive at the moment, but no more is the case as of now! Word got out that you're searching for the Sphere of Restrictions, which is something that the Zellites are not exactly the fondest of hearing about. But anyway... you're here now; I'm here too. I'm going to help you; I've already bailed you and the other one out.'

As he stated those last few words, Antonio stumbled on his feet, whilst pushing his hands outwards to maintain his balance. He appeared to be in a rather drunk and wry state with a tinge of exuberance, slurring his words ever so slightly. His shoelaces appeared untied as he continuously ran his hands through his hair whilst jutting out his chin, showcasing his perfect jawline. He was wearing a black business suit with a matching silk tie, gently smoothing out the wrinkles of his blazer, which had already appeared to be in perfect condition. Regardless, he clearly was well-experienced at maintaining assurance not only to himself but to others around him. Furthermore, he also seemed to be excellent at captivating people's attention, with his collective charisma and subtle charm, which already appeared to be working effectively on Florence.

Florence blinked rapidly and remained stern, holding a harsh, dismissive demeanour whilst suppressing the urge to cough. She was unwilling to evoke her weakened state in the presence of someone as influential and dashing as

Antonio. 'And where is she right now?'

Antonio smiled brightly again, proudly demonstrating his obvious expertise in the field of illuminating gloomy circumstances.

'Well, if you stick with me, I'm sure you'll find out!' He leaned forward sporadically and extended his hand towards Florence as she pulled herself up and dusted off the dirt from her tattered jeans. She nodded at him and smiled politely to express her gratitude and followed him out the door.

Chapter 17

Samira struggled to compose herself and experienced disruptive motions of sleep, her peaceful train of thought being wrecked with miniature bullets of guilt piercing her head. She tried to remain strong and resilient, but within disconcerting situations like these, where she only relied on herself to feel even a wistful scent of joy, it was sometimes better to do nothing at all.

She patiently waited for a glimmer of hope to arrive, remembering something that the Sage had mentioned to her hitherto the current situation. *The strength of your will is manifested within your choices and highlighted by one's actions.*

She looked down at her hands, her willpower and inner confidence wavering within her spirit.

'Samira? Samira!' Florence entered the room, knocking it open with her fists clenched firmly. As soon as she caught sight of Samira, she released them, pulling her up from the ground and embraced her.

'I have never been happier to see you again!' She smiled genuinely as her pale blue eyes brightened.

Samira looked behind her friend and noticed Antonio grinning and scuffling his feet against the ground, his hands relaxing inside his pockets.

'Who is this?' Samira whispered.

'Oh yes, this is Antonio. He claims that he is going to aid and direct us towards gathering more information surrounding the Sphere of Restrictions. He works for the governmental authorities aiming towards overthrowing the Zellites influence.'

'So essentially, I'm a rebel.' Antonio smiled and winked, leaning towards embracing Samira. Samira smiled uncomfortably.

'Pleased to meet your acquaintance. And what is your name exactly?' he whispered, matching the volume of Samira's voice and gazing into her eyes.

'I'm Samira,' she stated.

'That is a very interesting name. Samira... I'm assuming you have Arabian origins?' he asked.

Samira looked slightly startled and slightly offended at how this stranger seemingly believed that he knew everything about her despite only just meeting her now.

'Yes,' she stammered. She looked at Florence for a second, hoping to gain her support and signal her discomfort, but Florence appeared distracted by Antonio's apparent charm.

'It's OK; you are not necessarily obligated to engage in conversation with me. Come on, let's get started. Follow my lead.' He checked his Apple Watch for a second to check the time and began walking. Florence and Samira exchanged a look, both appearing slightly puzzled but continued following Antonio, nonetheless.

Chapter 18

Antonio dropped his phone abruptly on the floor and quickly bent over to pick it up, ignoring his little mishap and continued to walk away whimsically as if it had never occurred in the first place. The sky was relatively clear, with a few grey clouds towering over the group of three. A few minutes later, light drops of rain began pattering down against the surface. It was virtually invisible, not sulphur-infested, but rather damp and bleak. It emitted a strange smell that was almost smoky but not too distinctive.

Antonio looked behind at the two girls who were strolling casually behind him; he was the type of person who was easily bored when confronted with a situation that required minimal engagement. Hence, he was keen towards conversing with everyone else around him as a means of serving his own personal form of entertainment. As a former politician who had previously been discontinued from serving Parliament, he was now facing difficulties within his personal life, including an impending divorce after his wife had committed adultery against him, as well as striving to regain the idealistic reputation that he had once cherished and clutched onto as a source of affirmation and personal recollection. Politics was something that made him feel whole and worthy despite the inevitable misfortunes and corruption involved in securing one's position. But now, Antoniadis was an ally of a clandestine governmental organisation which had been set up by a near-distant friend of his to overthrow the Zellites influence and regain his reputation. He knew it wouldn't instantly provide a solution to his grave misfortunes, but it was a start. He was a strong believer in starting anew and regaining several chances in life, regardless of whether luck remained on his side or not.

'So, Florence, whereabouts are you from?' he said confidently, cocking his head to the side and attempting to win over her trust with a dashing smile.

'My parents are founders of a corporate business within the United States. Wynne Industries,' she mentioned bluntly, remaining composed and plodding forwards.

'Ah, Wynne Industries! I am familiar with that business! So, I reckon you must be loaded in that case?' He chuckled to himself, leaning over to her side and nudging her playfully with his elbow.

'So, you say,' she said, shrugging her shoulders indifferently. 'I see no bother about it; besides, it's no longer my inheritance anymore as they have now disowned me.'

'Why on earth would they do that?' Antonio exclaimed.

'It's a long story, but basically, I broke down and removed myself from that lifestyle, to put it lightly.'

'Yes, for an American girl, I must say, you are rather articulate in your expression.' Antonio pressed, his eyes shimmering ever so slightly, with a mild element of teasing in his tone.

Florence narrowed her eyes in disapproval, glaring at him, her nostrils flaring slightly as her brows furrowed. 'What's that supposed to mean?'

'I'm trying to offer you a compliment,' Antonio stated nonchalantly, remaining mellow and relaxed within his outward expression. He wasn't the type to easily advance an argument or any sort of conflict. While playing Devil's Advocate was relatively amusing for him, it often served as a disguise for his emotionally unstable personality, which he intended to conceal. He firmly believed that expressing outward vast arrays of emotion was illogical and ought to be discouraged by conventional standards.

'Well, thanks for the offer, but I've given myself enough commendations already.'

'Hmm... It's interesting how you are unwilling to let one's wealth define your current circumstances. I know people in demeaning situations who would readily attach themselves to a label.'

Florence paused for a second, trying to absorb Antonio's words as they exchanged a look and shared a silence that was relatively brief but, at the same time, felt rather long.

'What do you mean exactly?' Florence asked, lowering her voice a little.

'Power, wealth, influence, beauty, money, prosperity. That's what US citizens prey upon and desperately crave as a source of affirmation throughout their lifestyles. Without those factors, the ultimate dream or manifest destiny as such is non-existent and everything within its pre-eminent status that we have desperately strived towards accomplishing within history may as well be rendered futile and forever forgotten.' Antonio mentioned with a slightly wry smile plastered on his face, attempting to appear appealing and captivate Samira and Florence's interests despite showcasing a hint of insecurity within his body posture. Nevertheless, he arched his shoulders back a bit and ran his fingers smoothly through his hair, walking elegantly with unrestrained self-assurance.

'I like the way that you think, Antonio,' Florence mentioned, with a tiny smile forming on her face, whilst stifling a cough, which contrasted significantly with her previously infuriated state. As she stifled a cough she was slightly hypnotised by Antonio's explanation and outspoken demeanour. It wasn't something that she'd outwardly admit, but it was rather inspiring for her to see someone clearly mentioning and outlining what they think and actually acting out on their beliefs so passionately. Antonio somewhat had provided her with a fervent sense of reassurance.

Antonio turned to pay attention to Samira, who appeared to be rather dismal and detached, as her hunched shoulders slumped down and her head lowered itself towards the floor in a similar fashion.

'And what about you, was it, Samira? What do you value most in life?'

'I cherish my independence and self-worth above all things. Losing my dignity is enough to destroy my entire being. Everything else in this world may fade, but I cannot afford to be stripped of my ideals,' Samira murmured, emphasising the word *dignity*, as she continued to stare at the ground, reluctant to make eye contact with Antonio.

'Yes, I see. I would probably agree with that besides possibly giving up an entitled income.' He laughed, nodding at Florence, who coquettishly chuckled in response.

'Besides that, however, shouldn't we all be focusing on what is actually important here? Locating the Sphere of Restrictions?' Florence said, shifting the loosened underlying tension into a serious mood.

'Ah, yes! Exactly the item which rendered you lot imprisoned! Where must it be?'

Samira opened her mouth in response, but Florence quickly intervened. 'Actually, it's not an item as such but rather a type of vortex window which appears during your greatest hour of need.'

'Ah, so it's kind of like a TARDIS?' Antonio smiled amusingly at his own Doctor Who reference.

'Honestly, it could consist of anything; it may not even exist at all, just an entirely fictional concept or estranged myth which has been affixed towards our own versions of reality,' Samira mentioned, mustering the confidence to turn towards him, speaking directly.

'But isn't that the point of all art anyway, to render itself as an imitation of life? Designed to suit our own personal agendas, regardless of how they may appear to be? Because let's admit, at least one part of everything is superficial to some extent, right?' Antonio responded, challenging Samira's proposed thesis.

'That may be true. Yet, there is also a clear truth

revealed within every lie foretold...'

'Someone has a high level of awareness...' Antonio raised his eyebrows, accentuating his approval, appearing to be impressed at Samira's persistence towards winning an argument, whilst also leaning closer towards her curiously, failing to conceal his excitement at newfound insight expressed by her.

Florence looked down for a second with a hint of jealousy. 'Yep, you cannot dispute that.'

'Knowledge is drawn from the entity of wisdom; we only grow wiser through confronting our fears... I don't see why you have such an entrenched fascination with riches and material possessions,' Samira continued, ignoring Antonio's affectionate demeanour, instead giving him a side glance, begrudgingly as if his materialistic obsession was contagious.

'It's all a part of reaffirming my security. It may not be significant towards you, but financial expenses serve as the keystone towards restoring a sense of direction within my life. How could that not possibly matter as much to you?' he asked, raising his voice slightly in annoyance despite maintaining inquisitive interest.

'My faith serves as my greatest security,' Samira mentioned, half-frustrated, half-composed.

'I see... you surrender your bets and your fate to a greater power,' Antonio grumbled, shaking his head in dissatisfaction.

'Yes, and I see no shame in doing so. It forms a substantial part of my entire nature; without it, I feel weakened, weary and restless. Faith is the morning star that I follow whenever I am lost at sea.'

'You see, for me, it is the opposite. My faith only culminates towards greater chaos. Call it the supreme level of an existential crisis, if you may. I used to be like you, using spirituality as a means of gaining greater morality, serving as an enlightened source, encompassing my most heartfelt principles. However, I became burdened by the pressures of committing towards my faith and consequently focused more on its lack of clarity, which resulted in my impatience and impulsivity. I became unwilling to commit myself towards faith and simply obey. Instead, I longed to appeal to those within my inner circle, mostly following their own ideals, determining everything for themselves, feeling liberated by exploring their own identity and adapting the rules to see their liberal choices being manifested and generally approved. We lived predominantly in fear of oppression and potential dismissal by those in authority, discounting our integrity. Hence, I lost my faith in that respect. I was too afraid to commit towards something intangible. Thus, I believed that it would be easier to follow a pattern that would divert itself from attracting attention by unravelling even greater possibilities and opportunities made available to mankind. Of course, I will not be following the Zellites orders, practically forcing everyone to convert and exerting dictatorial force by threatening life. I'd rather affiliate myself with secularism, as that seems to be the most neutral stance in this polar battle. I never saw any other option... What even is the best option?' Antonio stammered, his voice quivering ever so slightly as his stable façade gradually began to crumble before their eyes.

'There is not exactly a "better" option to follow. What is most important is upholding a promise to yourself to do good by respecting and forgiving others, regardless of their beliefs. I see that as the guiding principle,' Samira whispered, sympathising with Antonio.

'And Florence?' Antonio looked wistfully towards her, allowing his walls to collapse and vulnerability to shine through his exterior appearance whilst remaining slightly hopeful in adoration.

'Faith is a complicated subject for me. One cannot be too sure of where their utmost faith stands unless they are faced with unwavering obstacles and challenging circumstances... I'm just waiting for that to occur at this rate. Nothing less and nothing more.' Florence hesitated for a second, drawing in a sharp breath to prevent herself from unleashing a coughing fit and walked swiftly past them, her expression remaining rather cloudy and distracted by an increased number of burdensome thoughts.

Chapter 19

Samira, Florence, and Antonio continued walking as the sun slowly began to set, leaving a stream of several shades of blue, peach, light crimson, rose pink, and orange merging together; leaving a glistening trail of mist aligned within the skyline as the streetlights surrounding them began to glow, lighting their path ahead. There were several travellers walking around within the mild temperatures of the hazy summer evening. The travellers were walking dismally with wavering uncertainty undisguised upon their faces as they prepared themselves towards potentially meeting their seldom fates without urgency.

Samira looked at them cautiously, with an unmeasured hesitance over succeeding in her quest, contemplating between hanging on the verge of fear or clinging onto ingrained perseverance. She was unsure about the harrowing circumstances likely to pervade her judgment as she gulped briskly, swallowing her sorrows and collective fears. If time remained on her side, surely any sign of the Sphere of Restrictions would have appeared by now? Surely, there was a reason for remaining dormant and stationary for a moment within time. She had now gathered her thoughts and attempted to maintain her cool, remaining ready for lightning to strike at any moment yet also patient towards extricating herself from any major or minor culpabilities.

Anytime now, she silently prayed. After stroking her hands to gain further comfort, she shifted her attention towards Antonio, intending to question him to relieve herself from the moderate likelihood of failing her assignment.

'And what about you, Antonio?' she asked firmly, as Antonio nodded towards her, with his hands remaining in his pockets.

'Yes, Samira?' he asked, raising his eyebrows and offering her a jaunty smile.

'Why exactly are you searching for the Sphere?' She scanned every inch of his body from head to toe, wrinkling her nose slightly.

'Why? For redemption, of course!' His eyes lit up as if they resembled candlelight flickering after a refreshing breeze had gone past. 'Locating the Sphere is my ticket towards serving our great country once more and providing somewhat of an antidote for our past misfortunes! Who would ever pass up such a rehabilitative opportunity?'

Florence and Samira looked at him, somewhat surprised yet half-heartedly supported his reasoning. Their search for the sphere may not directly resemble his own motives, yet they thoroughly understood the wondrous sentiment associated with attaining a second chance.

'That's totally fair,' Florence said, flicking her short hair back and grabbing her alcohol container from her pocket; she shook it slightly and looked inside for any droplets remaining, only to find none.

'Oh, darn it! I've run out of liquor!' She sighed, beating herself up internally.

'To fuel your inhibitive desires?' Antonio teased, leaning forward.

'That's something you've had your fair share of already.' Florence scoffed, pushing him backwards gently, rolling her eyes.

'You two should get a room,' Samira muttered as Florence's face flushed scarlet, giggling nervously.

'On a heavier note,' Antonio mentioned, digressing from the topic. 'How are we exactly certain that the Sphere will relieve humanity from this mysterious curse, sweeping mankind away? We've already had several serious pandemics; so, how can we guarantee that the Sphere will transform our lifestyles, eradicating poverty, disease, and all other sickly embodiments that the world encompasses? What if our time never arrives? What if we are not deemed worthy or esteemed enough to unlock the Sphere's potential? I mean, they don't call it the Sphere of Restrictions for nothing. How do we know for sure that we are granted access to it?' Antonio's hands began moving frantically, mirroring his disjointed internal mindset, with doubts and shortcomings and lost ideals swerving rapidly around his brain.

Samira looked at him seriously, her eyes peering intently into his as if she was trying to connect within the depths of his soul whilst also earning his trust and settling his acrimonious thoughts.

'There are limited boundaries possessed within

human choices to act rationally. For one's train of thought to halt for a second. One may possibly exert one's influence by believing that one is morally superior towards enacting such a pedantic, worthwhile action, only to realise that malevolent influences and consumptions of doubt divert one's attention away from a sufficiently moral basis. Instead, we become more attuned and inclined towards following our own selfish tendencies to remove further elements of choice, potentially hindering one's judgment. This is what ultimately leaves us restrained,' Samira stated, sighing woefully as Florence and Antonio gazed at her in awe, transfixed by this familiar revelation.

'And how does one deliver themselves from this mental confinement and emotional incarceration in an amicable fashion?' Antonio asked, his eyes widening as he delved deeper into scrutiny.

Samira adjusted her body posture slightly, raising her head up. 'One may fixate their attention towards human reasoning and further enlightenment through nature's divine inspiration. But ultimately, liberation can be attained by surrendering their malleable mindsets and seeking guidance from a higher power to attain absolution from their most sincere transgressions.'

'And how so?' Florence whispered in light confidence, presenting her subtle disbelief.

'Balancing the domains of reason and passion is proven to be essential towards receiving equanimity and solace within one's soul. One may feel naturally drawn and inclined towards these two pillars of the mind to exercise control based on their own personal counsel. However, we are not bound solely towards formulating a choice between thinking and feeling. It is this interchangeable restraint involved in sacrificing our heart's inclinations, in contrast to avoiding the rational regulations deeply entrenched within our own minds since the dawn of time. This is what deprives us from truly manifesting and emanating our authority within human existence. Whether we are satisfied or not, we cannot escape from experiencing the human condition without tactile emotion.'

'Oh, I am so disheartened! I have destroyed myself!' Antonio lamented suddenly, throwing his hands over his head and kneeling with agonising distress. He did not care at all about the other's reactions. He was instead overcome by shame and remorse; unable to conceal it any longer.

'What is the matter with you?' Samira scorned coldly.

'Nothing to concern you now! I am burdened by my past mistakes! I am wracked with guilt for initiating a war during my time as a politician! We decided to invade another country as a means of protecting our citizens and counteracting terrorism after enduring our previous bitter losses.' Antonio stared groggily into the distance as another man met his gaze and hung his head in deep regret.

Antonio paused for a second, whimpering bitterly and then continued explaining, 'I believed that I was doing the right thing by protecting my country from the pertinent inevitability of terrorism awaiting us. We had a multitude of resources presumably functioning in our favour. I thought of myself as the Saviour, resolving this imminent threat. Regardless, in reality, I could not be further from the truth. We had a multitude of resources presumably functioning within our own favour, with maximum security, as our technological systems were highly advanced. And yet, we still sent thousands of troops to die. Looking back retrospectively, we were far too rash. Our fear paralysed us so much to the point where we lost our right judgment. I do not even know why I should question my own reputation at this point. The loss of innocent lives at the expense of greater accolades is a much more damaging loss to acknowledge. I am still infuriated by the prospect of disposing of vital human resources, civilian integrity, and the like by initiating a war, serving as a major travesty of ascertaining peace through the predestined deception of mankind. We squandered and butchered everything that was good. For what? All for nothing.'

Tears began to splutter all over Antonio's cheeks as he whipped out his stained white handkerchief to remove them, sniffling solemnly as his face dropped further and his initial light-hearted expression had been exchanged by a gloomier forlorn appearance. His tone sounded increasingly startled and alarmed, cognisant of his own indiscretion. It was almost like observing a gigantic stone pillar, gradually destabilising and crippling its composure, internally and externally, fracturing its remains.

'Wow,' Samira whispered, 'mankind's abhorrence continues to scale to even greater heights! As we rarely ever rejoice. Instead, we mostly moan and create even bigger problems, stemming from our own abjections and insecurities.' Samira was rather horrified at Antonio's confession. She was bewildered and disgusted at the execution and perpetration of human welfare and security.

She was likewise perturbed by the clear violation of fundamental human rights principles, which had resulted directly towards the far-reaching annihilation and massacred intervention towards many innocent civilians. It was nothing more than preponderant decimation. She could clearly envisage how the legacy of such a diabolical event and purporting further blame continued to haunt and traumatise Antonio. It was more than enough to hurt anyone merely by hearing how pain and relentless sorrow could easily be transferred, with its immeasurable power impairing victims and survivors, penetrating all tranquillity whilst exerting colossal wounds with malicious insight and influence.

Florence crossed her arms and clutched them tightly towards her stomach, batting her eyelids in pure misery. Attempting to lighten the mood, she bitterly stated, 'Sometimes we're so focused on avoiding mistakes, we end up fixating upon further misshapen catastrophes.

'But perhaps our most misshapen catastrophes consist of our most successful triumphs. Perhaps through recognising our own fallibility and dysfunctional attributes, we become more receptive towards our ephemeral existence through humbling and surrendering ourselves towards nature's direction.'

Samira looked at Florence for a second and smiled to herself, gradually lifting herself out of the despondent fog which was beginning to evaporate. 'You're right, Florence. I remember how the Sage informed me about *collective responsibility*. Perhaps we ought to hold ourselves accountable for our own destruction as a necessity towards protecting the vulnerable and reconciling our own rights. Maybe that's how we can locate the Sphere?'

Antonio lifted himself from off the ground, with Samira and Florence's inspiration, igniting a glimmer of hope within his chest. Florence moved closer towards Samira and gently placed her hand on her shoulder. Samira glanced at the floor and then smiled back at her meekly.

'There's still time,' Florence mentioned in a soothing tone, conveying a relatively uplifting manner.

Antonio opened his mouth to speak until he caught sight of a squad of soldiers dressed in black, pointing guns directly towards them as if they were lethal targets.

'FREEZE! By order of law, we forbid you from moving!' they yelled in a menacing tone.

Chapter 20

"Seize the subjects," an elderly man who appeared to be the captain ordered, with his black robe ornamented with golden medals. He glared at Antonio, Samira, and Florence, as the trio glared back in response, absorbing the surroundings, taken aback by the action taking place. Florence coughed minimally, faltering slightly and almost losing her balance, as Samira held her waist tightly for extra support. The guards peered at her specifically, holding a condemning glance and moved in closer to handcuff the three individuals.

Antonio tried to wrestle against them and break himself loose, but the chains were as sturdy as steel, squeezing tightly against his skin. 'By order of the government, I command you to stop!'

The guards shifted Antonio and the others into a dark, black van located behind them as they sneered at him and laughed maniacally. 'Who put you in charge? We only follow Zellite Law!'

Samira sighed in depletion, feeling like something of less value than a pawn in a chess-playing field of knights and queens. Of course, the Zellites were behind this abrupt capture. They were masters at bending the rules to suit their own private agendas set towards harassing the public through concocting volatile desires. They primarily instigated chauvinistic *ideals,* intentionally harming the marginalised within society, as if they weren't already bearing enough hardship. They were also incredibly inconsistent within their beliefs. For instance, they intended upon eliminating anyone who would threaten the disposition of their twisted worldview conceptions. Despite representing the "people", they would act in accordance with the antonym roots of democracy. Moreover, anyone who acted in compliance also had no chance of securing enough income for their own families. In Samira's eyes, renouncing yourself to untrustworthy authority was like walking lackadaisically into a cesspool consumed with despotic desires, with a stark deprivation of expressing autonomy or any definitive promise of release.

*

Upon exiting the vehicle, which had only reached its destination within five minutes, Antonio, Samira, and Florence were stripped of their possessions and strapped against a gate, with their hands bound tightly against the gate with a spiky wire protruding from it in all sorts of directions like thick thorns prickled all around a black rose. The sun remained absent as dusk had hit its peak. Antonio looked up and sighed heavily in frustration after his several attempts to break free remained futile. Samira felt inevitably uncomfortable, scanning her surroundings to find a reasonable solution or tool to aid them, but she also discovered no avail or definitive measure providing any necessary means towards their escape, despite their efforts. Florence looked down towards the ground and noticed a little grey stone beneath her feet with the words ingrained: *LIBERTY, FRATERNITY, EQUALITY.*

'Hey, look, check it out! It's a stone embroidered with the slogan for the French Revolution. Rather catchy, I might add!' Florence seemed particularly fascinated by the words encased upon the stone, pondering the symbolism of this strange occurrence. She had always restlessly sought to attain liberty throughout her life, despite constantly confronting externalised expectations imposed by misleading influences. Nevertheless, throughout Florence's adolescence, she had garnered enough courage to bloom and flourish and to become complete within herself, enabling the opportunity to fully articulate and acknowledge her own desires through self-expression. However, she felt lonesome within her parents' shadow, in addition to dealing with the solitude of being an only child without any siblings backing her up or even teasing her around to succour her spirits. As a young child, her father often reminded her about her societal role. She was obligated to appear appealing, dainty, and polite to further accentuate the family image as though she was the model of civilised beauty. Her father would remind her that it was paramount for her to continue doing so to feel galvanised and receive inner graces that were destined to make her stand out from the rest of the crowd. Thus, throughout her adolescence, Florence continued maintaining an image which showcased her sense of affinity and empowerment, often intimidating other individuals at the expense of displaying her own power and potential. She would do this in a manner which strongly resembled her elders, in fear of dismissal or perpetuating disarray. She had never regarded herself as anyone's equal. Instead, she had previously believed, (before enduring her own private psychological battles), that she needed to display her own individual supremacy and preconceived puissance over others to assert her self-worth in equal measure to satisfy settled standards for public accountability, security and self-affirmation.

Likewise, Samira also found herself mesmerised by the words affixed to the stone. For something of virtually no practical value and so miniscule within the colossal landscape of creation, it certainly upheld a significant message for all individuals to follow. She had once believed that liberty was priceless, until she later realised that the price of liberty often fell at the expense of one's affirmability, reputation and overall appearance within a human landscape. In fact, from Samira's perspective, liberty was an element within the grand scale of life, most affordable for the rich. Hence, for the destitute, the isolated, the most forlorn and impoverished souls, liberty was inevitably so much harder to instantly grasp.

Yet, from an alternative perspective, they seemingly were also the freest without any possibility of crippling doubts evolving and financial concerns coming to light. Instead, everything that man constantly strived earnestly for would no longer be an issue for them. Every potential whim of instability could be evaporated. Whilst Samira was thankful for financial benefits due to her disability status, offering her with enough stability to last within the course of her lifetime, she would also question if it was also somewhat of an apology from society surrounding her inability to live in accordance with normal expectations.

Regardless, she never intended to brashly instigate further harm upon herself simply because she'd always be perceived in an alternative manner, requiring greater attention or less. What comforted her most was that she was not alone in this. Either way, in some form, everyone was in some way dysfunctional or lived a decrepit lifestyle with a range of deficiencies, and this did not necessarily consist of an external form. Often, the most profound struggles were invisible to the naked eye. It was something that Samira realised that rendered us all equal. She contemplated the viability of human nature clinging onto even a thin wisp of authenticity. As she continued to staring at the stone, pondering about humanity's desperation to conceal their struggles, she felt even more disconnected from reality. Eventually, her mindset drifted towards being chained against a gate between two individuals she had only just encountered a couple of days ago. She was utterly perplexed about how she entered this situation in the first place. But then again, life was accommodated with endless surprises.

Antonio, after remaining quiet and seclusive within his own mangled, entrenched thoughts, finally began to speak again after yawning. He often struggled to remain quiet for long. Besides the Zellites, liars, murderers and hypocrites, boredom was his worst enemy.

'I am so tired and fed up with this. They definitely

should have a reasonable explanation for this; otherwise, the Council will be hearing from me, and then those crazy, deformative excuses for human beings will come to their senses, justice will prevail and—' He paused abruptly as a viper slithered past nearby whilst five Zellite soldiers began marching their way towards them.

Chapter 21

'You know, you should really learn how to shut your mouth when you get the chance.' A middle-aged Zellite soldier hissed at Antonio whilst smirking menacingly and leaning upright against his face as a means of asserting greater intimidation. He was rather broad and bulky and spoke with an almost unintelligible accent.

'Oh yeah, feel free to bet against it,' Antonio said whilst casually imitating the soldier's accent in the process. 'Why don't you attempt beating the odds?'

The soldier laughed and then slapped him hard across his face, leaving a burning reddish mark on Antonio's gleamingly bronze skin. Antonio looked down as his glossy dark hair brushed over his forehead, wincing in pain slightly. He then looked towards the soldier, glaring at him vindictively.

'You really are useless, vain and weak,' the soldier muttered parsimoniously as Antonio rolled his eyes at the typical cliché villain line.

'Why don't you display some human decency and let us go?' Florence intervened, with an equally aggressive tone, her eyes likewise narrowing down at the soldier, loaded with fury as if there were hidden bullets locked inside them, ready for release.

The soldier turned towards her, responding bluntly,

'You sweet, pathetic little girl… Not a chance.' He met her gaze without even a hint of remorse or sympathy. He was iron-cladded with ice, completely void of displaying emotion as if he was immune towards feeling any form of compassion or agony. Florence coughed mildly and grunted, totally disgusted by the sordid sociopath's ignorance.

The soldier continued talking whilst walking around, gloating with a lofty sense of pride. 'You know, delinquents like you never respect the law. You never respected our rituals. You never believed that we were doing everything within our power in *order* to protect you. In *order* to offer you the best opportunities in life. To transfer only the purest genes to your offspring so that they may also rejuvenate, abiding with the correct law. To become the gold standard of humankind. An epitome of utter perfection, outshining the rest and becoming a beacon of light and hope for all to follow. But no, you don't care for the worth of others. You'd rather waste your life causing nuisance and disruption towards us all, terrorising us with your rebellious nature. You really think that you're above us all. Well, you thought wrong, and look at where it has rendered you.'

Florence smirked at the soldier's gallantly foolish depiction of dramatic irony. For someone who spoke rather fondly about maintaining order, his thoughts could not be more disordered.

'Actually, if anything, I'd be questioning whether you believe that infiltrating and brainwashing the minds of innocent lives, with your corrupt and incredulously devious schemes, has done anything in particular to promote the goodness of humankind?' Florence questioned with enflamed confidence.

The soldier snorted in return. 'As if you have anything to offer yourself, my darling! Petty damsels like you don't deserve the right to speak, let alone work.' Florence sparked up in anger, gritting her teeth and restraining herself from swearing as she did not want to paint a poorer image of herself than the derogatory misogynistic filth firmly fixated within the soldiers' minds. Florence hung her head in a mixture of disgust and devastation, appalled at how people believed that it was OK within their right minds to not only think but explicitly belittle others by stating those exact or similarly crippling words.

Antonio's eyes flared, angered by such a comment. 'You know, there is a word for people like you. Or maybe more than one. Cowardly. Ungracious. Ignorant. Deluded. Oh, wait, consider those as understatements… In fact, I'll just be honest and say this plainly without hard feelings: People like you sicken me, and I'm a politician; that's enough to put anyone off.' Antonio smirked, whilst his green eyes remained deadly serious as Florence smiled, flattered by Antonio's means of defence.

The soldier moved an inch closer towards him, lifting up his clenched fist as a cold breeze entered their external surroundings, rushing in at an outrageous speed, unleashing grandiose gusts of air, chilling their spinal cords, and eventually swirling around them.

'What by Heaven and Earth is going on?' Florence stammered, merely petrified.

The wind gradually picked up greater strength, bashing harshly against the chains that were tying the trio to the gates in an ultra-supernatural fashion, leaving a cloud of white smoke, gathering collectively within their vision as Florence, Antonio and Samira broke free. The dust continued to swerve and swirl around them until it circled entirely around Samira whilst blue light protruded from the skyline, shining a dazzling light and radiating its tranquil essence as it sprinkled and descended onto her. The arrogant guard ran away frantically in terror, dispersing like a tiny replica of fluff leaving a dandelion clock during a hurricane.

Samira, appearing dazed and losing her balance, collapsed onto the ground, extending her fingertips and limbs as she felt suffocated by the thick air surrounding her whilst simultaneously stunned by blazing follicles of light, extracting every essence of energy, draining her entire system. After a few seconds, it stopped, permitting her to stand once more until a loud, rambunctious sound excreted from afar as the wind picked up and swirled around her rapidly, whipping her around as she felt nauseous and dizzy, holding her breath and then panting slowly.

She stood there, aimless. With an open heart and a subsisting spirit, she gradually lifted her eyes upwards, staring intensely towards the endless void of the midnight sky. It was towering above her like a grandiose collection of jewels, formulating their own separate constellations, intertwining and culminating within a metaphysical connection. An accumulation of the forces of nature were leaning beside her until suddenly, a gentle pause instilled within her. She continued to stand as a combination of rays of light and convergence rapidly extinguished her vision. 'It's not time,' she whispered to herself, desperately trying to comprehend her immediate lack of control. 'IT'S NOT THE RIGHT TIME!' she exclaimed and kneeled on the floor resembling the verge of oblivion, bursting into a bitter cycle of tears…

After composing herself for a few seconds, processing her ineptitude amongst the tremendous omnipresent collective forces beyond all human power and comprehension, she opened her eyes. Only to realise that she was once again submerged in darkness.

Chapter 22

'Samira, do not feel perturbed. We're right here beside you,' Florence whispered, kneeling beside her, attempting to alleviate her crestfallen spirit.

Antonio sighed. 'You said it's not the right time. What did you mean by that exactly?' he asked curiously, remaining serious.

'My eyesight, it's weakened... my newfound abilities... they're fading...' Samira stuttered, struggling to compose herself and convince herself about the despondent truths facing her. She brushed her hands against her thick, long hair as a means of gaining even a minimal amount of control.

'What if my hearing withers too? How will I be able to complete my mission?' She started shaking, stricken by panic and immense doubt, unsure about whether her fading abilities resembled her failure to complete the task set out for her personally or whether the time barrier may finally reach an expiration, leading towards further disintegration into her formerly disempowered image.

'That won't happen,' Florence mentioned boldly. 'Because you will always be able to lean on our support.' She smiled at her affectionately and sneezed whilst Samira tried to muster a smile back.

Antonio looked at her in intriguing disbelief. 'Wait, so

what you are trying to say is that she was blind this whole time. Or formerly so? I'm lost.'

Florence gently tapped his elbow and faced him. 'Samira is actually a paraplegic; she was gifted with regular abilities of able-bodied citizens to support her throughout this mission set by the Creator.'

'Oh, how bizarre yet delightful!' Antonio exclaimed as the pupils within his eyes dilated after absorbing and comprehending this extraordinary phenomenon.

'Don't feel too ecstatic. This poses serious obstacles within our mission. We must stay focused and alert at this time, now more than ever.' She gazed at him intently whilst raising an eyebrow. Antonio cocked his head slightly but then quickly nodded in approval and continued walking ahead.

'Yes, yes, let us continue.'

Florence picked Samira up and assessed her feelings; Samira nodded, affirming her reassurance and conviction that everything was in control with the insistence to continue moving forward. Samira sighed as they continued walking, with the wind stroking against her coarse, bristly hair until they reached a tree to rest by for shelter and to catch up on sleep after escaping and being liberated from the fortress.

'I'm going to head north for a bit to adjust the compass' coordinates. I would prefer it if you both left me alone.' She picked herself up and turned to face them but failed to look at them directly as she was unable to see with total clarity any more or even visualise their possible reactions. She realised within that moment that she needed space to reset her mindset and come to terms with her own senses in isolation again, without further distractions, to fully process and nurture her own personal relationship with herself. Despite everything, she was primarily accustomed to solitude and maintaining solidarity through reckoning and gaining strength within her most dismal moments. To fully recover from this temporary recess, she needed time to adjust towards her surroundings alone, dealing without typical senses, which others would often take for granted. She brushed her feet against the thick grass below her, with sensations from the ground guiding her and granting her stability.

'Are you sure? You've just lost your sight! You don't have to do this alone,' Florence stated, her tone resonating with a highly concerned dictation.

'Florence. Leave me be. Besides, there's still time.'

With hesitation, Florence nodded, and Samira wandered away, with her head hanging low, overloaded with her disjointed thoughts.

Florence remained calm, intending to flick away any further concerns regarding Samira's dejected state as rapidly as possible.

'So, what would you like to do now?' she asked Antonio, smiling weakly.

'Well, we may as well just wait for something to happen to us by doing nothing. We've already done enough; I don't see much more of what we can possibly do.' He shrugged, fixating on the field in the foreground of their vision.

Florence chuckled as she gently pushed her light hair

back and stared solemnly at the ground. 'Well, passivity may be a choice, but it's not the only choice. I wish that we could do something to help Samira, but once again, we're rendered powerless within this giant playing field resembling life.'

She turned and coughed slightly whilst Antonio leaned towards her in slight curiosity. 'Is everything all right? You keep coughing every now and then.'

Florence inhaled sharply with a blank expression. 'I'm surprised that you noticed.'

Antonio shrugged casually. 'I guess it's always awkward to comment on these sorts of things; I'm presuming that you have some sort of asthmatic reaction? Or are you dealing with something else?'

Florence looked at him again. She hated giving in and admitting her weaknesses, but it was hard to conceal her true nature in Antonio's presence. 'I have a rare terminal disorder. I've had it throughout my whole life. And honestly, I have no idea how much longer I must survive. I've already crushed my inhaler as well as pretty much every possible chance of sustaining my life.'

'Really? You feel as though you've butchered your chances?'

'Yep,' Florence mentioned, attempting to conceal her despondence, yet a slight hint of sadness still managed to seep through.

'Well, I admire your resilience,' Antonio admitted with a hint of sarcasm.

Florence flared up abruptly, 'Oh really? So, you've never suffered enough or endured so much mental and physical affliction leading towards you giving up everything that you have? You haven't been willing to sacrifice everything for the sake of gaining eternal peace rather than forming commiserations with your past mistakes and affairs without any potential for closure?'

Antonio scoffed. 'Please, I don't need your drama. And I'm not going to give you any form of false pity; I've had my fair share of all those. I know what it's like to feel bent on giving everything up. Besides, we often attain more power in situations where it is certain that there is nothing more to lose. It moves us towards acting irrationally, out of spite, out of vindication for all the wrongs that the natural world has sought out and unleashed against us! But despite it all, we're encouraged to never give up, to never lose hope, to never renounce our pride or self-individuality. And yet, it can easily be stripped away from us in an instant. As soon as we sense even an inch of weakness within our systems, we crash and burn. Our entire mindsets freeze and turn frail! And then we become reluctant to admit or accept any form of defeat. From everything that I've grasped from you, it sounds as though you want to die.'

'You can make as many assumptions about me as you wish. But wouldn't you agree with me that dying is something that we have all wished for at least once in our lives? Whether we are suicidal or not? Some people wish to die to become reunited with their beloved. Some people wish to die to escape insufferable, never-ending pain. Some people wish to die because they are too afraid of continuing to make meaningless, rash decisions if they continue to live. After all, what is life without the impending certainty of death? The whole prospect and inevitability of death reaffirms life's existence and yet is something that we continue to feel afraid of, jeopardising our own chances of living naturally as a consequence.'

'So, what is it that you really want Florence? Would you prefer to die out of nobility, gaining control over your own death without seeking medical treatment? Or would you rather die after consistently living in fear with a lack of control over your gravest concerns? Feeling completely vulnerable and powerless over your destined future?' Antonio stood up, looking down towards her, his face remaining as hard as a stone.

Florence wheezed and exhaled, letting out a deep, chesty cough in the process, standing up to face him with her hands crossed against her stomach for support. 'Who do you think you are? No matter what our circumstances are, it is not up to us to decide who lives or who dies. I've been abandoned by everyone in the past who I believed seriously loved me. I've been betrayed by friends who had previously done everything within their power to protect me. And yet, here I stand with a choice to face even more horrendous repercussions from my diminished standard of life, without individuals or finances to uplift me or even provide minimal support throughout my anguish. Or I could choose to continue living, submerged within misleading certainty and wavering insight, alongside my fatal condition. And yet remain hopeful that everything will work out for the greater good,' she mentioned boldly, loosening her arms and wrapping them tightly against her stomach whilst expressing melancholic sighs.

'Well, let me make this decision easier for you, Florence.' Antonio scowled menacingly as he whipped out a sharp pocketknife from his suit and thrust it suddenly into Florence's abdomen.

Florence gasped and screamed out in excruciating pain as she thudded onto the floor, dropping onto her knees.

Meanwhile, Samira had commenced heading her way back towards the spot under the tree where Florence and Antonio were. However, after hearing Florence's blood-curdling screams, her eyes widened in astonishing alarm as her skin flushed cold, and she ran towards her, mustering all the speed that she had left whilst holding back tears.

Chapter 23

Samira held Florence tightly, cradling her in her lean arms. Florence had shifted her position and remained lying helplessly with her back on the floor, relying upon Samira's support and resting in a slightly upright position in a desperate attempt to gain more oxygen, whilst Samira dabbed onto her wound with her tunic to compress the remaining blood tissue as Florence shuddered and sputtered out heavy clots of blood, bleaching her delicate white skin entirely with masses of dark red liquid.

Florence wheezed with tears streaking furiously down her face, almost as in an attempt to eradicate every little emblem of pain shrouding her internally. To no avail, she continued grunting and breathing as the colour continued to drain from her face, complicating the process of purified oxygen cleansing her system and recklessly evaporating the last remaining limbs of life-sustaining her.

Meanwhile, Antonio towered over both girls shamelessly.

'Why would you do this? I thought that you cared about her. But you're nothing more than a spineless, deceitful excuse for a human being!' Samira yelled explosively. She felt overwhelmed and consumed by heated rage, which led towards her hands quivering uncontrollably as she turned to face Florence again, pleading desperately for her life to be saved.

Antonio continued to stand firmly, his eyes narrowing slightly. 'I did it out of love. It was her wish.'

'Taking a life is unjustifiable by any means. How could you have no shame for exercising such an inhumane act of falsified mercy?!' Samira wept bitterly.

'Suit yourself! I was only expressing her best wishes and granting her further autonomy!' He snarled.

'How could it ever be possible for her to exercise her autonomy if she's dead? If anything, you disrespected her choice and used it to your own advantage! Decisions like these should never be up to us!' Samira scolded aggressively with a vicious tone spewing from the tips of her lungs.

'Your aggravation is getting to you. You are deluded! There's nothing that you can do to prevent her suffering and there's nothing that you can do to safeguard her life either. If anything, supporting her is only going to destroy her even more. Besides, you're both nothing more than lost causes.'

'Leave! Florence doesn't deserve to hear anything like that right now. Hatred will only lead towards more hatred; you've disrupted the course of her life enough! Just leave!' Samira hissed, unmasking the monster that was brewing up within her system after listening to Antonio's despicable last words.

She frowned ferociously as Antonio shook his head and fled, never to appear in sight again.

Samira quickly focused her full attention towards Florence. 'Florence, I need you to survive right now.

Please, we've come too far to find each other to lose each other again,' Samira stuttered between each word, overcome with fervent disbelief at the tragedy occurring in front of her.

'Samira, it's OK. I need you to continue without me. Besides, I had reached my expiration date already. This was meant to be.'

'No, I will not accept it. We'll find effective medical support and then we can both locate the sphere of restrictions. You can make it. You will make it! We cannot lose each other. We need each other. This isn't happening. I need you to live.' Samira remained stricken with tears, which had been fully exposed for the first time since she had encountered Florence. She had been successful in maintaining a stoic demeanour as much as she could throughout their whole journey together, but the prospect of losing Florence, a girl she genuinely loved and admired, was only little of what was required towards her complete sabotage. It only took an ounce of her pain to tear her apart.

Florence gazed into Samira's eyes and whispered. 'It never was about locating the Sphere; it was rather the divine privilege gained throughout every interaction with you. You know that our friendship will outlast all restrictions.'

'How much we all long for the damage that we have caused to be enough...' Samira responded. 'The magnanimous love that we shared should make everything all the more worthwhile, collaterally.'

Florence smiled as her eyelids shut, and she drifted off into an eternal slumber. Samira stood up and briskly turned away, unable to find any motivation to remain still with her fallen friend. So, she walked away, within a dreary silence, with her mood as sullen as the grey sky above.

Chapter 24

Samira continued walking away, towards an orchard, to find more fruit to eat, completely disarrayed by the unsatisfying truth that she was once again isolated alone. She had never felt more infuriated in her entire life. As the image of his obscene act continued flashing within her mind, Samira believed that it would be better to completely erase him from her memory, but that was so much easier said than done. She was beyond appalled by Antonio's betrayal. In fact, she had always felt a negative intuition surrounding Antonio, almost like a premonition alerting her towards avoiding any possible interactions with him. She had encountered several people like him before. People who would say all kinds of things about expectations and enacting ideals, yet who lacked the courage or commitment to fulfil those duties in accordance with others' best interests. Instead, they preferred to stick with their own "safer" agenda.

Regardless, she felt further dismayed within herself. If she had been there before to support Florence and had remained by her side before the deadly deed had been performed, she could have easily prevented it. But instead, she was obliged to bear the consequences, lamentations, and reckless regret, alone. People like Antonio disgusted her. She was baffled at how it was possible for presumed friends to establish their loyalty for a reduced amount of time. This form of betrayal would shift casually elsewhere in a swift motion without providing the perpetrator with a chance to fully process or even displaying genuine signs of disapproval towards their flawed sense of judgment.

As she continued strolling, she desperately tried to obliterate further waves of doubt and denial surrounding her friend's demise. The guilt was draining her tremendously as the strains of sweat trickled down her face, and the overall humidity of her surroundings intensified. She hadn't known Florence for a long time, but the time she encountered and felt blessed to share with her made up for the countless times she was unable to relate to anyone besides herself. She realised that life consisted of multiple seasons, composed of multiple opportunities for transition whilst revelling within the joy of connecting with individuals which we never believed could uplift ourselves prior to that one moment of meeting.

But above everything, she felt immobilised as her withered spirit was forced to deal with a significant loss. She could not comprehend the reasoning behind individuals left with the remains of their beloved. Moreover, she was aware that the memories prevailed against every other tragic circumstance, transferring gratitude and bliss towards something that no longer existed within a lifetime was an impossible task. Yet she knew certain instances in which only Florence was deemed capable of reacting could be foreseen as irreplaceable. The connection between them permeated against the intangible lines separating the notions of life and death.

No force instigated by humankind could be rendered capable of reversing misfortune, removing her heartbreak or restoring her crestfallen spirit. Yet, at the same time, new seasons were paramount towards reverting her weary mindset back towards a more illuminated state. However, she desperately needed the strength to distance herself from a state of stagnancy in order to accept the possibility of renovation.

After strolling dismally for a few hours, Samira decided to rest by a fountain which caught her attention. She took a sip of water from it, cupping her hands to collect the particles as well as using it to bathe her arms as an attempt to cool herself down and engage with its therapeutic essence. She wondered how Florence would approach the situation that she now found herself in, vice-versa, had Samira been murdered by Antonio instead. She wept, quietly wishing that she was taken in exchange for her place. She often pondered upon the reasoning regarding why certain people lived and why certain people have been swept away from existence. But questioning the motives of the Divine Plan often burdened Samira with greater worrisome thoughts, which would only satiate her madness.

As she braided her hair with her vision remaining poor, yet her sense of sound remaining intact, a grandiose, dazzling stream of light rippled from below the surface of the water streaming underneath the fountain and burst upwards, with a multitude of colours consisting of violet, cyan blue and streaks of silver shimmering and converging into a large circle of light enshrouding the entire atmosphere. People nearby continued to watch, dazed and overpowered by this seemingly identical recreation of an amorae-specillis, with crystallised spectres of light floating around and emanating authentic sentiments of tranquillity and serendipitous attenuations perpetuating forces of settled composure and pure peace.

Samira squinted her eyes as a woman with a glistening white gown embroidered by moon pearls, which appeared to be dancing across the intricate, immaculate designs of roses carefully sewn onto her dress. Samira gawped in disbelief to realise that even within the midst of her pure vision, the Sage had appeared visibly in front of her and touched her shoulder to extend her deepest sympathies and condolences for Florence's loss.

'Why are you here?' Samira whimpered, 'I thought that I had failed my mission...'

The Sage looked at her in total adoration and smiled contentiously, 'Who clarified the fact that you have failed your mission, Samira? If anything, you have never been closer towards attaining success!'

Samira frowned, confused and taken aback by the Sage's enthusiasm and good compliments. 'I'm not sure whether you can recall, but I am currently mourning the loss of my friend. I'm renouncing my role in this mission. Whether I have failed or not, this has all proven to be futile. I'm done.'

Samira turned away from the Sage, who remained standing with her feet in the fountain, yet her long dress somehow remained dry. She stepped out and began to follow Samira as Samira continued muttering and cursing.

'You know, I brought this onto myself. I decided to follow and befriend Florence. I decided to leave her with that awful excuse of a human being. If only I hadn't been consumed by my feelings of solitude and had instead focused more on the danger that surrounded me, she would be at my side right now, emboldening me with the confidence to continue moving forward. But now I am stationary, unwilling to move, incapable of reversing the course of time. Instead, I am ridden with guilt and shame and agony and the repercussions of leaving my greatest friend behind, now deceased.'

'Samira, you must not transfer the blame onto yourself. After all, you did not destroy her life; if anything, you tried to ameliorate it. As individuals, we do not possess the ability to give life itself but rather to restore the innate brokenness through our intimate connections. You and Florence will always remain intertwined within the same spirit, regardless of life status.'

Samira remained still and sat in silence for a brief moment, allowing herself to process the discomforting truth merged with the Sage's admission. 'But why couldn't the Creator save her? Why was I left alone?'

The Sage looked at her intently. 'To do so would disrupt the pattern of free will. Where one's will is free, one gains the strength to circumvent any illustration of poor choices. Antonio had made his choice; the reasoning behind that is only known between him and the Creator. I know that you cared for Florence, but his transgression and judgment are not of concern to you. For now.'

Samira remained silent, resisting the urge to lash out all her frustrations, complaints and lamentations surrounding Antonio's undeniably diabolical behaviour. She was aware that for many merciless criminals or psychotic cold-blooded killers, who remained innocent for a while in their lives, would often surprise the world with remorseless behaviour permeated by sickening injustices and heinous acts against humanity. She wondered how brittle or twisted one's mindset must be to resort to such a low level and find pleasure in destroying lives - rather than taking the initiative to rebuild themselves from their own deteriorating self-sabotage and ill-fated destruction.

As much as law and order intended to restore civilisation towards its further greatness, it would always fail to control the nature of moral choices exemplified by mankind. She knew that individuals would often build fortresses of protection out of their finances through extensive national security to prevent the violation of their reputation. Their derelict behaviour remained desperate enough to construct walls of deceit to deter others from enacting in accordance with the principles of true justice. And yet, it would never become possible for such individuals to completely escape from their own fears or imminent sources of danger, even something as tiny as a bite from a bedbug. Nothing ever really remained secure.

The Sage gazed longingly at Samira, unable to fully decipher her thoughts but was certainly aware of her extremely high level of distress. 'You know Samira, you once mentioned that a person's solution is not dependent upon being influenced by various individualised levels of morality but rather is showcased by their willingness to search for the right answer in the first place. What would you deem as the appropriate measure towards seeking the right answer within this moment?'

Samira's vision blurred as she dismally sighed and stared at the ground. 'Florence would want me to continue; she'd want me to fight. But I don't believe that I possess the strength to do so as of now.'

'I see...' the Sage responded, 'however, Antonio has killed one of his own; that is the gravest offence against humanity. He will be condemned for the rest of his life if he fails to seek repentance or even gain your forgiveness. Forgiveness will grant you the grace to continue. The Creator desires for your forgiveness as much as how he likewise endlessly forgives.'

Samira blinked a few times, remaining silent until she stumbled upon an encrypted message below ingrained within thin calligraphy, organised into horizontal lines, lined symmetrically against each other, slabbed subtly onto a piece of a flintstone.

'What is this?' she whispered, her eyes widening as she attempted to read the message aloud, very slowly, absorbing every word that flowed:

What is love?
Love easily falls, yet true love is difficult to find.
Love is a powerful force that connects humankind.
Love is mysterious, dangerous, and bold.
True love is never weak, frightening, or cold.

Love is a fascination that leads to obsession.

As its overprotective nature and passion may cause destruction.

Yet, love is ultimately a sacrifice, a liberating gift.

Love allows every small feature of the universe to shift.

True Love is found in inspiration and connection.

True Love is regarded as the image of perfection.

Love is fragile and delicate yet incredibly strong.

Sometimes, love is still there, although it may not last for long.

Love is profound admiration,

which can be unlocked throughout a deep conversation.

True love is permanent despite life sweeping it away.

Love can be frustrating and could end in dismay.

Love is a vicious cycle filled with extreme emotion that causes commotion.

Yet love is also as clear and colossal as an ocean.

Love is an intrinsic piece of human existence.

Love has no boundaries or a set distance.

Love may seem like nothing,

But unconditional love combines and consists of everything.

The Sage nodded. 'Yes, it is the exquisite beauty enraptured in human nature and divine law that unites us.'

Samira reciprocated the Sage's nod and extended approval. 'If forgiveness is the only thing which would render my soul durable, I will continue to move on with a merciful heart.' Samira dabbed her tears whilst smoothing her hand over the stone and gazed solemnly into the distance.

Chapter 25

The sun had fallen as the midnight sky was overshadowed by dark violet hues, swirling across the atmosphere. The horizon above was dusted with red velvet wisps, as little stars speckled around, twinkling in the set distance. Meanwhile, droplets of rain had also begun to fall lightly, as Samira's hair dampened and straightened slightly in the process. She was ambivalent on deciding whether to be frustrated by the dismal setting or not. Usually, she enjoyed the occurrence of rain, washing away her sullen spirits, yet she simultaneously wondered if it was conducive enough towards mustering the possibility for her to refresh her perspective so that she could ignore the fact that her closest friend was no longer beside her. She had also lost track of time, unable to gather her thoughts collectively to understand her status or the requisite steps required to finalise her mission. The mission that she was no longer ready or willing to complete. Despite the personal trajectory that ensued within this journey, she was growing impatient, especially as she was practically certain that there remained no chances of any improvement. She had gone back to square one but was now levitating within her own apathy. Yet she begrudgingly continued against her own will as she had no idea what else was destined for her besides attaining further struggle and disappointment.

The Sage walked towards her and tapped her lightly on the shoulders, intending to elevate her spirits. 'Come, quickly!' she exclaimed, 'There is still more to be done.'

'What more is there possibly to be done? I don't see the Sphere of Restrictions! I'm tired of believing in anything seen or unseen. I know I said that I will aim to become more merciful. But if you expect me to reach a stage of perfection as of now, then you're only deceiving yourself.' Samira turned her head away, tugging her tunic, which was now incredibly dusty and slightly tattered as she had spent a couple of days without cleansing herself.

'Actually, before you continue with the Creator's mission, we may as well get you cleaned up,' the Sage mentioned, beckoning Samira towards following her to a hidden cavern secluded below the surface from where the two were standing.

As the Sage urged Samira to follow her down the footsteps onto a dingy path, Samira's bones began to grow weary as she remained insubordinate to the higher power attempting to reform her. The Sage held onto her tightly, almost like a mother endearingly cradling her new-born child, as the two stumbled into a grand bathing room, with the temperature starkly contrasting towards the previous chilling night air. As Samira examined her surroundings, she beamed at the spectacular and gloriously evanescent location. There were bathtubs on both sides evaporating hot air and bubbling up further streams of purified water, intermingled with a lavender scent, permeating the atmosphere. It was almost as if she was in direct contact with paradise, only luring her in further and shielding her from any potential nefarious force bent on wrecking her. Instead, she instantly felt at ease and mildly satisfied for the first time in a while. As she sat down on a chair to rest and bent her head down, dozing off to sleep, the Sage stripped her off her garments, which were now incredibly tarnished and streaked with coal, with a nauseating stench lingering from them as she set them aside gently. She then grabbed a portion of camomile oil and spices from a wooden bench below and slowly massaged and rubbed the lotion all over Samira's body until a waxy glow was visible. She then found a medium-sized laced dress and attached it to her, zipping it up carefully and smoothing the edges over to provide further comfort. Samira tilted her head to both sides, smiling peacefully to herself and yawned. Whilst opening her eyes, she unravelled her tight, deepest brunette braid and loosened its grip, running her fingers through her hair, which was now curly and damp with coiled locks.

The Sage noticed that Samira was awake and consoled her whilst stating firmly: 'Before you meet the Creator and locate the Sphere; it is absolutely essential for you to convert yourself.'

'A conversion?' Samira whispered, glancing at the floor for a second. 'You never mentioned this before.'

'I know, but at the time, you were so disconcerted, and in a panic-stricken state, it only would have increased your level of distress. Instead, you needed time to adjust to your newfound state as a means of confronting your most paramount concerns, whilst strengthening your willpower to combat them. A believer's journey is never going to be easy, but you have proven yourself worthy to offer consolation towards those who do not believe. So, now it is time for you to pledge allegiance towards divine inspiration. For the Creator has destined this path for you, but you need to willingly guide yourself towards following his route.'

Samira simply nodded, unsure about what more to add to this predestined plan and instead decided to concede as she somehow felt enticed into doing so, inexplicably. The Sage moved her towards the bathtub and pushed her head with minimal force onto the surface of the water, which was rippling in a motionless manner; it remained still yet continued to flow at the same time, as if time had ceased for a couple of seconds but continued to progress elsewhere. She lifted her head out of the water, opened Samira's clenched fists as the water was rather chilly and brushed Palmer's oil across the palm of her hands whilst stroking a horizontal line across her forehead.

'Henceforth, you will be known as Amira, meaning "*daughter of nobility*". Will you accept the Creator's plans for you?' the Sage declared, her vocal cords remaining potent.

'I accept,' Amira mentioned, staring straight ahead and, for once, not thinking much about the potential consequences or scenarios resulting from her brash decision. Rather, she remained focused yet docile, uncertain about the future, whilst embracing everything that could possibly be.

Chapter 26

Amira turned her head away, smiling modestly at her own reflection. The Sage had now faded from reality once again, meaning that Amira was now the only person standing in the room. Her vision continued to be unstable, but she was still capable of hearing and walking. She may have strayed far from the most supreme idealistic version of herself, but she likewise acknowledged that it was vital for her to sustain her gratitude for having possession and autonomy over her other abilities in comparison to where she had begun throughout her early life. She had always been familiar with the phrase *"coming-of-age"*, but she never had given herself a chance to genuinely contemplate its meaning. For instance, she had encountered many adults who were envious of young children for living out their childhoods without serious commotion or the daunting prospect of attaining insecurity. She had heard many adults commending children for living out their freedom and making the most of it before it would end too soon. Yet, at the same time, she knew of many individuals who had lost their innocence at a young age, fleeing their countries after living with the consequences of active conflict and the cruel devastation of loss associated with outlandish displays of violence, insolence, and rejection, eradicating every glimpse of blissful joy which had been previously sealed within their comforting childhood memories. Amira also remained aware of how young individuals longed to grow up faster to escape their restrained lifestyles. She also understood that they were unable to think freely for themselves, so they would prefer to discover their own passions, take giant leaps of faith and expand and explore their own horizons without the fear of the unknown hindering their inquisitive mindsets.

Yet for Amira, coming-of-age meant nothing more than accepting death. Accepting how vulnerable, powerless, distraught, and finite we all are. Accepting the fact that power, entitlement, resources, and riches are only temporary issues, no matter how transformative or dominant these material assets may appear to be within our lives. We may continue to consume ourselves with an excessive amount of priceless possessions which are presumably most precious for ourselves, only to realise that they would never fully eliminate our disappointment.

Amira also knew that pride would always remain as our greatest hamartia. We would always actively incite conflict or commit crimes to elevate our own forlorn, twisted sense of potential, to galvanise a form of ultra-superiority which would render ourselves untouchable, without realising that doing so distances ourselves and makes the prospect of earning true respect and acceptance even more inaccessible.

Likewise, we had deceived ourselves into believing that love will never be enough to promote harmony. Instead, all our futile efforts towards showcasing our own pride by diminishing others' worth and sense of dignity would continue to deprive us of living justifiably within the present. Yet, in spite of this despotic pandemonium, Amira needed to believe that change was a possibility as she refused to remain trapped within mankind's fallen state. She was reluctant to encourage humanity to remain forever fallen.

With a heavy sigh of relief, she was on the verge of leaving the room as suddenly, an overbearing spectrum of violet light flowed through and floated upwards as Amira peered her eyes closer towards the light, unable to fully process the complete image, as she was swiftly uplifted by a swirling spiral of air, drifting her meticulously into an unknown abyss. A gentle breeze and a crescendo of various sensations, as well as angelic choruses stemming from soprano and ranging towards mid-alto and mezzo-soprano sounds, pushed her further into the light. Her position then became rectified as the overwhelming force pummelled her firmly onto the ground, which was surprisingly soft as the sound settled down, ceasing until she was again overshadowed by silence.

Before Amira knew it, the walls surrounding her narrowed as her head smashed against the surface, and she lost her balance, and became concussed. Yet, she quickly regained consciousness as a medium-sized lump on her head began to swell. She rubbed it slowly, attempting to ease the swelling and rapidly looked around the room, which was rather blurry, but she could cryptically observe grid lines resembling a vortex, carefully aligned and barred in a complex manner, as her jaw dropped in astonishment.

'Amira, I am beyond delighted that you have finally

found your way...' a toneless voice mentioned. Amira could not locate precisely where the figure or being or person was situated, yet she could feel a refining warmth and affection, soothing and assuaging her heightened senses.

'Are you... the Creator?' Amira stammered with her olive skin tone becoming visibly paler.

'I can sense your distress but do not feel perturbed. My presence has always been instilled within you and will continue to be instilled within you if you allow it to do so,' the Creator responded in full tranquillity.

'So, this is it? The Sphere of Restrictions? So, I've completed my mission?'

'Not precisely.' The Creator chuckled. 'In fact, you must continue; your mission officially ends once you have taken your final breath and left your ephemeral state.'

Amira continued to stand stunned and significantly overwhelmed, unable to respond in a dignified manner.

The Creator spoke again, easing the tension, 'You see this orb...'

Amira looked up and noticed a medium-sized dark royal blue crystallised orb as clear as stainless glass appeared abruptly in front of her. She looked at it, with significant attention, as her eyes fixated on its internal colours fluctuating languidly like butterflies on a hazy summer's day.

'Yes,' she whispered.

'This is a representation of the Earth, the idealised Earth without imperfections. I intend to make a new Earth in conjunction with paradise at the end of time, one where suffering will cease to exist. How that will become your reality, however, remains a mystery…'

Amira gulped as she smoothed her hands over the orb and held it carefully within her hands, staring at it directly for a couple of moments, remaining silent. Whilst doing so, little cracks began to protrude within the orb's glass surface, enlarging gradually, until it exploded, as shards of glass shattered onto the surface and vanished rapidly.

Amira, however, continued kneeling in solitude.

Chapter 27

Daybreak had now become visible as Amira found herself outside once again on a palm beach. The grains of sand embedded themselves onto her soft skin as she stared at the ocean, where the tide was laying low, discreetly out of sight. Amira maintained a grave composure, gazing solemnly at the ocean's surface as she tried to relax and calm her turbulent thoughts. She continued looking forward until she heard footsteps as a middle-aged man, cleanly shaven, with his brown hair tied neatly into a bun, approached her.

'Hello, it's such a pleasure to make your acquaintance!' the unknown man mentioned smiling boldly. 'I am Ahir, the Elder; I see that you have made contact with the Sphere of Restrictions.'

Amira turned to face him, remembering that the Sage had informed her about Ahir when she first embarked upon the mission. 'You are indeed correct. I was conversing with the Creator, and he showed me an orb until it smashed, and I was transported here. I have no idea what my next steps consist of… and yet he told me to carry on. I expected the world to reach a stage of recreation or for humanity to receive its Final Fate and yet nothing happened. He just told me to continue.'

'And that is exactly what you must do, Amira.

Continue everything as normal. There is still time.'

'You all keep mentioning that. But how does time continue to exist when people are dying every minute? How does time continue to exist when natural disasters aren't ending? Why is it that we can never say enough, and everything will suddenly halt, or we can just choose at which point in our life journeys to end a chapter? We have the power of free will, yet that free will does not contain the power to dominate over time! We are given dominion over the earth but not time. How is that so?'

'Sometimes, when we get caught up in our own personal concerns; we forget that we didn't exactly create ourselves. Because of that, we cannot exactly choose the precise point at which our lives will end. That will continue to be a power unknown to us. But your time here really counts, Amira. There is no point in getting distracted by potential solutions that will always remain out of our grasp. Your most dominant ability is located within your current reaction. You may not know specifically the hour of which the Creator decides to transmit the course of time into another dimension. Yet, you are free to go out and continue educating yourself and those around you of his divine benevolence. Remind people that they are never alone, continue to spur on, illuminated by hope, mercy, love and gratitude. The blind may continue to lead the blind, but whoever carries the true light transfers that same light onto those who likewise discover themselves through unleashing and witnessing the proof entailed within divine inspiration. Your will may falter, but there remains a chance that it will solidify righteously. In the end, it is paramount that you must somehow strictly convince yourself that all things will work out for the greater good.' Ahir smiled at her reassuringly as he sat beside her on the sand.

'I understand. Even within the shadows of my despair, there remains a strain for goodness. But how can I possibly avoid being confined by those who wish to harm, diminish, and persecute me?'

'By trusting that every situation that once occurred has emboldened you with extra protection against the wicked snares of death. Evil is only authorised by the wilful agents of those who intentionally filter out any remaining recourse of benevolence.' Ahir sighed, continuing.

'The ultimate measure of reality that defines humanity as both shared between and limited amongst all of humankind is the ability to suffer. Suffering renders us insurmountably equal regardless of our confining circumstances and individual possessions that may be handed to us by fate to our own detriment. Unconditional love is ultimately the only force that exists among us without restrictions. It is an **unlimited** force. Once we combine this with our imagination, it becomes fully accentuated and remains the only possibility towards attaining our redemption and form of personal freedom. Through seeking love and genuine acceptance, we become more capable of truly emancipating ourselves from any circumstance diminishing our abilities.

Do not fall victim to deceit and false ideals; they will only leave you astray until you fall into the clutches of darkness.'

Amira nodded in acceptance. 'It will not be easy, but through constant faith and utmost attention, I will aim towards averting myself from malicious influences. I will always naturally be flawed as much as any other person, regardless of my condition, but my elders once encouraged me to continue to grow and to never allow others to dim my light and full potential. One is limited by knowledge. One is limited by ability. One is limited by wealth. Yet, we are all conjugally limited by pain.

Regardless of where we are within our journeys, what we have already faced, or where our fate lies, we are bound to be affected by life's multiple fluctuations arising amidst perpetual limitations. The imbalance within our current society holds formidable power, which can only be stabilised by hope. My predominant hope for humanity is that we will continue to prevail over our own tempestuous temptations and grievances by simply accepting the compassion which we unconditionally uphold. For this compassion remains intrinsic towards our own existence and will lead us towards our immutable destination.'

'See, you know what this Final Battle consists of. That is what the Sage meant by defining you as the last Samurai. There are millions and millions left, yet you are the last remaining... There may be millions left to fulfil their own part; but right now, you must focus and continue enlightening others around you.'

'But there are thousands of other people like me left out there! How can such a grand duty be designated to solely one individual?' Amira exclaimed.

'With time, you will realise that fate is not only up to you to decide, but rather... For you to simply accept.'

Ahir stood up and left her alone without saying another word. Amira remained on the beach, meditating upon everything that Ahir the Elder had mentioned to her. She was aware that she ultimately possessed control over defining her role, which did not necessarily need to be as prominent or excessive as implied, but she knew that it began with obedience. She realised that she needed to continue discovering more about her surroundings whilst retaining her authenticity.

With her lips sealed tightly, she gently lifted her head up towards the boundless sky above. Her eyes widened delightfully as she allowed the surrounding air to draw her closer towards liberation. Her body remained bound by the earth whilst her soul roamed freely. The passionate agent dwelled instantaneously whilst glowing and growing, uplifting her spirit. Within her ceaseless silence, the indivisible fabrications of the Creator's essence enveloped her heart entirely. Looking up towards the clouds, she reached forward, emboldened by unwavering courage, compassion, and confidence. She surrendered herself and succumbed to the light in accordance with attaining full fortification.

At last, Amira became enlightened by a refined and recalibrated mindset. Renewed and rejuvenated once more, she graciously raised her hands in adoration, remaining minuscule within the grandiose depths of the Creator's majestically exquisite works of art. Waves of nostalgia swept across her mind as she wept jubilantly. As streams of sunlight swayed and tilted in a supernatural fashion, glimmering and glistening with nothing more than its stark, iridescent radiance, overpowering the shadows lurking below. Instead, the superiority of its luminescence continued transcending against the unfathomable remnants of further exploitation on the surface.

Within Amira's eyes, death was regarded as the inevitable limit and consequence of original disobedience. In addition to this, she remained conscious of the potential threat and endurance of further harm occurring. Nevertheless, she acknowledged the possibility of establishing true peace within suffering, which reinforced the likelihood of reconciliation. Above all, she believed that the hope of salvation would remain intact and present for eternity, towering above imminent despondence, igniting her innate senses, and leading her home.